VENGEANCE OF THE VIGILANTE ROLLER SLUTS

A novella by

Gregor Cole

And born rabid and frothing from:

And an excerpt from Gregor Cole's latest:
PICKLES: ClownCunt. Pg: 103

~VENGEANCE OF THE VIGILANTE ROLLER SLUTS~

This *shit right here* is a **<u>MorbidbookS</u>** blunt. You dig?

Morbidbooks. Everything Bleeds.

Chapter 1

Sonny's teeth smashed into pieces as his face bounced off of the edge of the sink. Blood pissed out over the white porcelain and across the mirrored walls of the ladies toilets.

The tall blond girl with an eye patch stepped over the whimpering heap of pimp on the wet floor. He started to shiver with fear as she grabbed a fist full of his hair on the back of his head and dragged him into one of the cubicles.

"Fuck my little sister in that arse, you rat bag piece of fucking shit!" She screamed in his face. Then she proceeded to smash what was left of his mouth into the black plastic seat.

She flipped the lid and stuffed his head down the bowl while pressing her knee-high stiletto army boot into the back of his neck; she pulled the flush chain.

The half-conscious man gargled as the rush of the cigarette butt filled water flooded into his lungs, sending him into delirium. His arms waved for a few moments and he spluttered and choked in pure panic. His body went into spasm then he flopped like a dead fish on to the sodden floor as his oxygen starved brain shut down; his head still jammed in the toilet.

There was a click and a flash of steel as the busty girl with the eye patch shoved the blade of her flick knife up the prone man's anus. Sonny didn't even twitch from the thrusting insertion of the knife.

Sonny was dead.

"Fuck you, Sonny; fuck you up your stupid fucking arse!" The girl hocked up a huge ball of phlegm, rolled it around in her mouth for a moment then released it into the bowl of mashed head, splintered teeth and bloodied water.

Two curvy girls, one red head, one brunette, were sitting on the sink making out with each other as the blond left the bloodbath cubicle. Splatters of crimson started to be absorbed by her already soaked army shirt.

The hands of the girls were inside of each-others zip front grey boiler suits and they sat in the blood from where Sonny's face collided with the surface. The brunette had a finger smear of it next to her mouth.

"You two sluts put each other down and go tell Moira that Sonny's done. I'm coming in, just got a little business to attend to first."

The two girls jumped to attention with a crack of sixteen roller skate wheels on the hard tile floor. They straightened themselves up; wiping away saliva and smudged pink lipstick; zipped up their clothes and teased their hair back into shape with black glossed finger nails.

The two girls sounded off in unison, "Yes sir, Sergeant Tea-pot." As the two started to leave the big blond grabbed the shoulder of the red head and pulled her back.

"Not you Fire-Crotch, all this fucking blood has got me going." She started to unbuckle the belt on her camouflage hot pants. "Down you go, bitch!"

The brunette in the boiler suit ripped through the rain damp streets, the wheels of her skates almost smoking from the speed.

Screaming past the rude boys at the chicken shop, the Arab off-licences, the Russians out front of the gym; not even the Nigerian taxi drivers had the balls to fuck with one of Moira's roller-sluts.

She hung a left into the yard of *Bald Boy Roy's* junk yard and headed for the archway lockups.

With a leather gloved fist she banged on a door in the railway bridge; a small flap of wood opened inward and two oriental eyes peered out, then the flap closed.

The sound of chains and locks released behind the peeling blue paint of the door clicked and rattled and the smell of thick incense wafted out as it swung open.

The brunette stepped in past the oriental girl dressed head to toe in a black rubber bondage suit and high heels; the girl nodded and closed the door.

The roller-slut glided through the long hall, passing candelabras and racks of S&M equipment. Then she drew to an abrupt stop, the bright pink toe stopper squeaking on the smooth stone floor.

Moira stood proud.

Black rubber gloved hands on her curvy hips, her huge breasts held up with a strip of gaffer tape that ran around her body like a boob tube. She wore a lower body suit that had horse's hooves at the feet rather than boots that run into the rubber leggings. The black rubber slick with water-based lubricant and a massive strap on cock bobbed in front of her.

She swept back her raven black hair and spoke with a sultry Scottish accent that could get a eunuch hot. "So, Little Miss Rocket, did Sergeant Tea-pot get the bastard?"

"She did, Mistress Moira." Little Rocket bowed her head and realised there was a male gimp strapped to a sun lounger behind her Mistress, his buttocks exposed and well oiled. "She hung back with Fire-Crotch, said she had business in town, Mistress."

Moira started to jerk off the thick rubber cock jutting out from her hips and she licked her lips. "Yeah, I bet I know what business she has."

She turned to look at the human fuck toy sprawled out on the lounger and smiled a wicked grin. The gimp looked towards the brunette on skates, fear in his eyes. Rocket smiled back.

"Do you want to join me, Rocket?" Moira shot a sly look over her shoulder to her young apprentice. "I need someone to hold his fucking head; this cunt does love to fidget, so."

Rocket giggled with delight at the offer to watch a professional at work, if she was lucky she might even get to plate the mistress and sleep in the big bed that night.

~GREGOR COLE~

The little brunette rolled around to where the gimp's leather clad head was and she unzipped her grey boiler suit. She pulled each skate free from the suit without slumbering to reveal her tight body. She stood over the gimps head and started to lower her well-trimmed pussy and tight round arse, pinning the slave to the lounger.

But, just as Moira came up behind slave, evilly eyeing the man's hairy lubed hole; lining up the dildo for a deep plunge, the doors of the lock up burst from a huge explosion.

Shards of splintered wood and a thick cloud of dust filled the great hall and it was all the women could do to dive for cover in time.

The Oriental girl on the door caught the brunt of the explosion; parts of her started to land in great brunt lumps on the stone floor; each piece landing with a wet slap. A huge section of the archway door smashed into the gimp; he had no chance at all being trussed up ready for the fucking of his life. It split the poor bastard in two.

Little Rocket managed to stay conscious just long enough to see the hall swell with well-armed police in SWAT gear followed by men in long beige rain coats. The pigs were raiding the safe haven of her mistress.

Rocket tried to get up. She used all her strength to try and stop the armed men from dragging her mistress away but was far too shell-shocked from the blast to do any good.

~VENGEANCE OF THE VIGILANTE ROLLER SLUTS~

The last thing she saw was a flash of bright light as a policeman cold cocked her with the butt of his rifle. There was a sharp pain in the front of her head then blackness, nothingness.

She was out for the count.

The cop that smashed in the brunette's head stood over her. He looked down at the sweet pale nakedness of Little Miss Rocket; feeling a twitch in his dick. Just as his hand started to rub his slowly swelling member his captain barked the order to shove her in the van. It made him jump as the command broke his lurid fuck fantasy.

He would get his chance back at the station, the cheap little slut.

Count on it.

Chapter 2

Sergeant Teapot left the bathroom adjusting the belt to her hot pants and looked back over her shoulder. "Don't wash your face, bitch. I want you to taste my pussy all the way back to base."

Every person in the *Queen's Legs* public house were gaping at her; considering what they had just heard coming from the shithouse it wasn't surprising. The brutal pulverisation of a man followed by ten minutes of girl on girl orgasm wasn't something the average sleepy out-of-town boozer was used too.

The tall blond strode through the full bar like she owned the place, every head turned to follow her, each face agog with shock. She turned to the barman with an evil smile that made his blood run cold and his dick throb in his pants.

"Black Russian, large and plenty of fucking ice," she said, "and I'm taking the glass with me." It was the first time she had ever seen a barman pour a drink with his mouth open in awe.

She eyeballed the rest of the patrons staring at her around the bar and shrugged. She lit a thin black cigarette, blowing the smoke in the face of an old man sitting otherwise placidly on a stool next to her.

The bartender finished making her cocktail. He shook almost uncontrollably. He handed over the drink with fear in his eyes. The lumps of ice rattled inside the glass. The bartender flinched when she slammed a five pound note on the bar-top.

"And, if you call the cops," she added, "I'll be back in here to make a purse from your ball sack, fucking worm."

She slinked away from the bar and wiggled her hips out of the door followed by the roller-slut, Fire-Crotch. The red-head slapped the shaking, gawking barman across the face. Then she blew him a kiss as she rolled behind her mistress and out the door.

An old man at the end of the bar broke the silence. "What the fuck was that?"

Outside Teapot straddled her custom 450 bobber with the disabled parking motif painted on the fuel tank. The bike throbbed between her long legs as she revved the engine and strapped on a Nazi Storm-Trooper helmet. *Safety first*, she thought, smiling to herself.

Fire-Crotch zipped up to her side to receive her orders.

"Join your little slut partner at base and report to Moira." She spat the cigarette out onto the wet ground. "I have business in town." She downed the last of the drink and crunched the ice cubes between her teeth.

"Are you visiting him tonight, sir?" Before she could see it coming a sharp backhand caught her hard across the cheek.

"What the fuck's it got to do with you, bitch?" The mark on the girl's face started to rise up quite fierce, red and warm. "Now do as I say before I flush your fucking head down the Kermit."

The bike roared off into the drizzly night as the roller-slut stood and watched. Her pussy was tingling from the session in the toilet but more now from the slap around the chops. She successfully fought the urge to touch herself as she rolled through the streets.

She turned in the opposite direction from her mistress and flew off to join her fuck-buddy back at Madam Moira's. Her urge was squishing between her legs as she skated away in long, leggy strides.

The heavy military style high heels clipped and clopped up the vast stone steps of St. Denis Catholic Church. It's ornately decorated architecture topped off with a statue of poor old sod Denis himself, carrying his own severed head to his watery end. A stained-glass window of a decapitated head in a basket has backlit the morbid monument beautifully.

It was late night confessional for the local down-and-outs. Father Billy extended the olive branch but it was seldom taken up.

A few homeless types sat on the steps quaffing super strength lager, wolf whistling as Teapot passed. She took the wind from one of their sails when she stamped on the tramp's bollocks. The piss-head let out a whelp of pain before passing out. Teapot used the last glugs of beer from the tramp's can to *anoint* the other wasters, throwing the can at them. Then she continued her climb.

The huge wooden doors loomed over Teapot and a lump started to ball in her throat. She had never liked walking through these doors. Even as a child she found the place sinister.

She removed her trooper's helmet and let untidy blond hair flop free. She straightened her eye patch then slipped inside the building.

Inside was a little different. Here a warm glow came from the hundreds of candles that were lit all around the huge building. Teapot stopped to light one herself, adding her little bit to the overall glow. She said a little prayer herself then crossed over to the confessional.

The place stank of bag-lady. One had apparently pissed on the floor while sleeping. Her pathetic collection of rubbish stashed under one of the pews. Teapot didn't stop to harass her; this was a house of god. She thought that she might wait outside, and then set fire to her in the street. If so, Teapot would spend a little time later pondering the lady tramp's death.

As always at this time of night, the confessional was empty. She double-checked to see if she was followed. Once clear Teapot then slipped into the booth and closed the curtain.

"Forgive me Father for I have sinned," she began. Her eye remained closed and her gloved were hands clasped at her chin.

The priest behind the veil's voice was low and gentle, "Speak my child, let god hear your sins."

"I have killed tonight. Then I had improper relations with a female companion."

"Dear god, continue my child. Unburden yourself."

"I smashed a man's face in; he had wronged my family. I killed him with this knife." The blade clicked open and the priest on the other side gasped. "And I killed him real good, too," Teapot added.

~GREGOR COLE~

"Please my child, save not my blushes," Father Billy encouraged the roller-slut. Please, spare me no detail."

"Well, after I drowned him in a toilet I stuck the blade up his backside and turned it."

"Oh my god, child, what did you do then?"

"I forced my apprentice to lick my pussy over the body."

"Did she do a fine job of it?" Father Billy asked. He was getting a wee bit breathless. He loved the confessions of roller-sluts.

"Well, her tongue probed my wet cunt, deeper and deeper and she pushed a finger up into my arse…"

"Right, right. I see, my child." The veil between the priest and Teapot flew open and a thick veiny cock thrust through the partition. "It is time for your penance, slut."

"Oh my, Father… what is this?" Her voice thick with sarcasm as her fingers closed around his engorged rod.

"Put it in your mouth you little slut, and I'll wash away your sins with my load."

Teapot bent to stuff the cock into her mouth when the A-Team theme tune started to emit from the back pocket of her hot-pants.

"Fuck!"

"Don't fucking stop now. For your forgiveness is nigh."

"It's my family, I have to." Father Billy groaned his disappointment as she hit *answer* and pressed the phone to her head. To his delight she used her other hand to stroke the priest's *bishop.* "This better be important," she said. "I'm in the middle of something."

On the other end was an out of breath Fire-Crotch. She explained that Moira's had been raided and that she was hiding in a burnt-out car in the wreckage of the breaker's yard.

"The fucking pigs took Moira and Rocket then started planting huge bags of drugs all over the place, fucking cunts. What are my orders?" The voice on the phone rambled at a hundred words a second.

"Bastards!" Teapot gripped the dick in her fist hard with frustration. The priest on the other side of the confessional let out a faint yelp. "Wait for the filth to fuck off then round up the sluts," she replied. "I'll meet you out at *The Bunker* when I'm done here. Stay strong sister."

She hung up and slumped back into the chair, cock still in her hand.

"Was it important?" A caring tone in the voice from the other side of the wall tried to put her at ease. "Is there anything I can do?"

"Yeah, you can shut up and fuck my mouth, Father."

"If you insist, my child."

Chapter 3

Fire-Crotch curled up in the boot of the burnt out Ford Granada. She pulled a tarpaulin over her for extra cover and warmth. The tarp smelt of fish and fire and spunk. It was not comfortable. But at least the taste of her Sergeant's pussy still clung to her face. It was a heady cocktail.

From a gap in the smashed in boot lid she could see some of the frenzy outside through the now destroyed doors of the lockup. Police were everywhere. They had set up flood lights and cameras as the forensic team dragged body bags into the arches. A man in a beige coverall and dust-mask unzipped the long black bags to reveal smashed up corpses. He pointed to the rest of the team where he wanted them to put the bodies.

The fucking pigs were setting them all up and not just with dead bodies; other members of the team passed huge bags of white powder along a human chain into the hall.

Fire-Crotch fumbled for her phone and in the dark of the car rang Sargent Teapot to warn her of the trap that the police had set for anyone coming to Bald Boy Roy's yard. Teapot barked her orders but put Fire-Crotch's mind at rest. If anyone could sort this mess out it was the Sargent.

"Wait for the filth to fuck off then round up the girls. I'll meet you out at The Bunker when I'm done here. Stay strong sister." Teapots voice died away then hissed into dead air as she hung up.

She may be stuck but she could still act. Fire-Crotch started to text message the rest of the sluts that were nearby. Mad Molly, Sally Blood Fuck and the Gorilla were the only ones that were *Local 405.* Fire-Crotch started to franticly type; her long nails clicking on the touch screen.

Moira's raided, mistress M and Rocket taken
All to meet at the bunker ASAP
Don't reply just yet as am in a bit of a pickle!
Pussy kisses, F-C xoxox

Fire-Crotch hit *send* then made the decision to hunker down in her hideaway and watch the outcome of the raid.

Soon a procession of police vehicles pulled into the yard. Every person in at the scene started to clear away any evidence of any tampering. The lead car pulled up outside the blasted doors. A man in an expensive looking brown fur coat got out. He was followed by a fat man in uniform. It was Mayor Rodney and Chief of police Lloyd Felchman.

The fat man waddled around like some sort of spinning top. He was shouting at officers and pointing as if he had organised the raid. Fire-Crotch doubted that he even knew

~GREGOR COLE~

anything about the corpses or drugs that had been littered by the officers that he was now coordinating.

Suddenly an armed officer came from around a pile of cubed cars and walked to the back of the burnt out old Ford. He stood directly facing the boot where Fire-Crotch lay under the fucked tarpaulin. Through the gap she could see the officer unzip his fly and pulled out one of the biggest dicks she had ever laid eyes on; her mouth began to water instantly and a tingle started deep inside her sex.

The officer then let rip with a heavy jet of piss all over the boot. It was almost like he was aiming for the crack in the boot lid. Did he know she was in there? It was like he wanted to humiliate her, piss all over her, show her who the top-boy is. At least that's what she was thinking as the piss started to run through the gaps in the seals.

Fire-Crotch's hand slipped between her legs and started to rub the course material of her boiler suit against her vagina. A warm trickle of piss ran down her face. Her tongue flicked out automatically to catch a taste of the salty liquid on her cheek. Fire-Crotch was disgusted with herself but this was as close to a perfect sexual experience as she could think of and it was all she could do to hold back a moan and blow her hiding place.

In her head the officer flung the boot lid open, his still pissing member flopping about spraying her with hot urine as he pulled her from her hidey-hole. Fire-Crotch would struggle as best she could to stop him from hand cuffing her but he would be way too strong and easily overpowering. She would be in custody in no time.

But what if, she speculated, *the officer didn't hand her in? What if, instead, he raped Fire-Crotch in the old junk yard and beat her, left her for dead. What if he left her corpse in the boot of the old Ford so he could come back and defile her remains whenever he wanted? Come back and fuck her until she was nothing but a forgotten about puddle of rot and bones in the back of a burnt out car.*

A mind altering orgasm began to rumble inside the walls of Fire-Crotch's pussy but the sound of a zip being fastened and heavy boots walking away brought her out of her fantasy. He had gone, and she had nearly cum.

She finished anyway, trying not to make any noise. But if anyone had come within ten feet of the busted car, even in the gloom they would see it rocking. Old cars don't moan unless they are haunted.

Fire-Crotch didn't realise that she was asleep until she woke up stinking of piss in the boot of that car. She rubbed her eyes. Then they peered into the cold light of early morning at the crime scene. She was alone. Everyone had scattered to hell and gone.

Fire-Crotch gave it about half an hour before venturing out of the boot and into the frosty air. The boiler suit didn't give much in the way of warmth. She ripped the tarp into a makeshift cloak and wrapping it tight around, Fire-Crotch skated out of the yard, heading for the bus depot to get her out of town and to the safety of the bunker.

A bus picked up Fire-Crotch. She sat wearily down. An old lady stared at her from across the bus. Fire-Crotch knew she must have looked like the corpse of a dead whore found by someone walking their dog, but she didn't care. She did however care that she was being judged by a woman that last saw a cock when everything was in black and white.

Fire-Crotch just wanted to slap the turkey neck that hung from the dried up old cunt's chin. It retracted every time she breathed in.

"What's your beef, grandma?" The rough looking red head in skates and a green plastic cape asked. She leaned forward to better hear her riposte.

"Well I never. You are a very rude and filthy young woman. What's wrong with this generation?"

The red-head sat back, just watching the milky eyes of the old woman critique her every fibre, every strand of out of place hair, every streak of Fire-Crotch's smudged makeup.

A huge ball of spit flew from the full pink lips of the roller-slut. It spun and she watched it almost in slow motion as it crashed with devastating effect into the withered face of the sour old bitch across from her.

The old lady flapped her arms in a fit of panic and fumbled for the bus bell. The buss drew to a stop and the woman, still wiping the flob from her eyes and screaming, scuttled off of the vehicle and fell to the walk.

"And it's rude to fucking stare," Fire-Crotch spat at the hag again, "and I smell of piss by accident, you wrinkled old cunt!" As the bus pulled away she threw up a middle finger.

Fire-Crotch sat back in the seat and sparked the last of her cigarettes from a crushed box she dug out of her breast pocket. The rest of the bus was looking at her in disgust.

"What the hairy-ass fuck are you twats all staring at?" she asked, brusquely. "I suggest you all roll down your fucking shutters before I knife-fuck your eyeballs."

Sure Fire-Crotch had some anger-management issues. But she didn't like to be stared at.

Eyes were lowered.

Never underestimate the common asshole's ability to self-preservate.

Chapter 4

Father Billy chased the leggy blond down the expanse of steps as he buttoned his fly. He was determined not to let her leave on her own. Father Billy didn't want her riding to her death, not tonight.

"Wait, I can't let you ride into danger," he implored.

Teapot was already astride her bike and smoking. She didn't want to look at the priest for she knew her defences would crumble just as they did all those years ago.

"I have to help my sisters; my family." A thin black cheroot twitched between her lips as she spoke.

"I understand," said Father Billy, "but at least let me give you a ride. If the cops are framing you girls then they will be looking for your bike."

Teapot's lone pale grey eye almost burnt a hole through Father Billy's face. *How dare he suggest she leave her wheels behind?* But he was right; she would be next on the pig-list if they were taking people down.

Reluctantly she agreed and the pair pushed the bike into the catacomb entrance behind the church. Teapot wiped away a tear as they shut the heavy door. She didn't like the idea of her bike being alone in the cold dark.

Father Billy's car was a clapped out red Volvo with a blue passenger door. The car had definitely seen better days but who would pull over a priest in a rust bucket?

"Funds from the Diesis are light, no mod cons here." He cleared out some of the estate cars boot and folded down one of the chairs. It was just enough for Teapot to squeeze in to. "Pull the blanket and some of the junk over you, and keep down."

Father Billy reached in to an old army duffle bag stuffed in the back with the rest of the crap. He pulled out a sawn-off shotgun that was cut down to the size of a pistol. "Just in case someone other than me opens the back door," he said and smiled the smile she remembered from her childhood. The same malevolent grin he used to get whatever he wanted from poor unfortunate teenagers.

Father Billy sat in the front and leaned over to the glove box; inside was his disguise: a pair of thick spectacles with black plastic rims and a set of buck teeth that clipped into his mouth. He popped the teeth in and donned the glasses and looked in the rear-view mirror. This was the Father Billy that the general public saw.

His flock could not know the real truth behind the mild mannered cleric. They would not understand that Father Billy gunned down street gangs and pimps or that he took advantage of the older girls he took under his wing. They couldn't know the street name that preceded him with the town's *underground*. It is this dark underbelly where he stalked the cunt-peddlers and rapists.

The congregation of St. Denis simply would not understand. Father Billy knew full well that he would probably be de-frocked and left to rot in the streets. But he was the man that kept them safe at night. He was the twisted guardian that watched over them as they slept; a man who was not afraid to get his hands dirty. Father Billy was aka The Pimp Killer.

Their car trundled slowly through the wet streets of Cheap-Side. The pavements were alive with all manner of scum dealing and hustling one another, just trying to get over. Every man-jack one of them was searching endlessly for the come-up. But if any of them ever managed to find it, they would most likely blow the lot in no time flat. They'd be back on the street in no time.

There was no saving these people. Most of them were no more than rats in the eyes of Father Billy.

Every now and then there would be a glimmer of light shining out of the fetid shit like the one that was buried under the junk in the back of his car: Something pure, something innocent, and something trainable.

Father Billy didn't feel bad about what he had made Teapot into. If anything he had saved her, by training her to fight, to be strong and to protect the weak. He had made her.

"The man you killed tonight, it was Sonny, right, your sister's pimp?" For a moment there was no sound and Father Billy became anxious that she may have slipped out.

"Yeah," Fire-Crotch replied, "the fucking scumbag speck of dirt."

"And your sister, what is going to happen to her?" Once again a pause, like she was choosing her words, trying to hold back her temper.

"When she gets out of hospital she'll go back into foster care. They won't tell me where this time, so she'll probably disappear into the system." Fire-Crotch's voice was quiet and tired. For a moment Father Billy thought that he heard it break, fighting off tears.

The rain started to come down heavily on the shit box car's roof causing a sound like pebbles bouncing off it.

"If there is anything I can do," replied Father Billy in a small voice. It was his turn to pause. He continued, "I could at least try and track her…"

Before he could finish the sentence Teapot cut him off. "Can't this thing go any faster? Are we even out of the town yet?"

"Not yet. My wipers are shot to shit, can't see too good in this weather."

Teapot sat up. "Well if you took off those fucking geek glasses you'll be able to see."

"I have to keep up my persona," Father Billy told her. "If we get pulled over we might get away without being searched, as long as you keep your head down. All the cops know me here.

"Fuck that, Father." Fire-Crotch pulled the gun free of the blanket and climbed into the passenger seat. "I'm riding shotgun with you."

Even though this was a girl that he had reared from a teen he was still wary of her. After all, that there was an armed gang member sitting next to him. He was more than aware of what she was capable of. Just because she swallowed his spunk did not mean she would hesitate to taste also his blood. Fire-Crotch was the very epitome of dangerous and his back was turned.

His hand slid down the side of his seat to make sure his trusty .38 snub was still there. Just the feel of its cold steel and short barrel; its walnut grip, the feel of the hammer, was enough to make him breathe cooler, yet faster. As his thump brushed it gave him butterflies. The amount of low-lives it had spat lead at gave him a rush of adrenalin and his foot became heavy on the accelerator for a moment.

The idea of the sidearm just by his hand put his mind at ease, for the time being.

The bunker was out on a dirt road in the forest. An old biker-bar was tucked away from the world. It was a last resort for battle hardened gang members that needed a place to vanish. It was off the police's radar as they didn't have a licence to run the bar. It wasn't in any of the guide books. If the place doesn't exist, the police have nothing to look for.

The ramshackle tin-roofed cabin was originally built by a now defunct biker gang. The keys have been passed from crew to crew since the seventies.

Now Thick Steve had the keys. For all his short comings, and there were several, he kept his lips shut tight and the bar well-stocked.

Thick Steve was standing on the front porch when the battered Volvo pulled up the dirt road. His heavily tattooed arms were wrapped around himself, water poured from his thick brow onto his stained white apron. A crooked smile spread across his big face as Teapot jumped out and flung herself into a hug around the dopey man.

"How are you, pudding?" asked Thick Steve

"Better for seeing you, ya big fucking idiot."

"Go on inside, the others are waiting."

Teapot skipped up the wooden steps. She swung open the double-doors and waded into the stale smoke and the warm reek of beer and vomit. Teapot felt like she was relentlessly finger-banging sixteen year-old again whenever she came out here. It was the sound of the jukebox, the sound of people playing pool; such happy memories.

Thick Steve's expression changed when he caught sight of the driver. He had never liked the Father. He didn't like his church. Thick Steve had no argument for or against religion. He just didn't trust men that wore dresses. A heavy frown etched his face.

"Leave all religious stuff in the car, Father." He turned and trudged into the cabin. Out of the side of his neck Thick Steve said, "I won't have your god in my bar."

Chapter 5

Moira found herself in quite the pickle.

She was stripped naked and laid flat on a work bench in the centre of the cell. Her legs were folded back behind her shoulders into the oyster position. Her arms and head were strapped tight to the bench.

Usually people would pay to have this kind of service with her and whoever had done this sure knew their stuff. Moira couldn't move an inch.

The glare from the bare bulb overhead was bright and hurt her eyes. There was no escape from its glare even with her eyes closed. It just shone red light right though her eyelids.

Moira knew that torture was imminent.

The sound of distant footsteps rang through the basement. A key entered the lock of the heavy steel door at the far wall. Someone stepped into the room and shut the door behind them. Without being able to lift her head she couldn't see who it was. From the sound of the stranger's hard leather footwear on the hard stone floor it was probably someone important. Moira knew that she was in big fucking trouble.

"So you are the infamous Mistress Moira." A thick German accent echoed around the cell. "I am so glad I could have met you, especially like this. I have heard so many good things."

Even in her prone position with her pussy jutting out like a split football she held her resolve. Moira was adamant that if it was to be torture, she wouldn't break.

"Staying quiet? It's okay, I have all day and plenty of toys to get some sort of noise out of you."

The hard shoes clopped around the room, circling her, getting the measure of the busty fighting woman bent into a pretzel on the table before him. He was to have his fun but definitely had his work cut out for him.

The German knew that she had paid her dues as a slave girl on the BDSM scene. It was well known that Moira had a pain threshold second to none, but he had a few tricks up his sleeve and a selection of devices he had built for just such a woman.

"But I am being rude, Mistress." His head suddenly loomed over Moira's face, backlit with the single light bulb. His dark, slicked-over hair caught the light like a halo. His pencil moustache twitched as he spoke.

"My name is Dr. Lars Walpurgisnacht, but you can call me Dr La-La," he replied, smiling wickedly at her. "I am here to keep you entertained."

Rocket's eyes flicked open as the rain got heavier. She sat up to find herself in some kind of containment yard surrounded by storm fencing. She still had her skates on.

Rocket's hands were cuffed and chained to the floor. The guard that had cold-cocked her was now standing triumphantly over her. He was pointing his gun at her head.

"You awake now, little bitch?" The guard barked.

"Yeah, I guess," she replied. "It's either that or I'm in douchebag hell."

The officer stamped in a puddle just in front of Rocket, slashing a great wave of the cold water into her face. She had no doubt that it was *a next time the boots in your face* warning.

"Thanks."

"No problem, fuck-whore."

"You keep calling me names and you're going to get me hot, big boy." She shook the water out of her eyes. "And why am I still fucking naked?"

"The captain thought you wouldn't try anything stupid if you were left bare-pussy." The guard moved closer. "And if you scratch my back…"

~VENGEANCE OF THE VIGILANTE ROLLER SLUTS~

Rocket's eyes rolled. "Let me guess; I blow you and you take me inside and get me a towel and some hot coco."

"Bingo!"

The doctor whipped a sheet covering another bench on the back wall to reveal a selection of insane looking devises. There were bundles of PVC straps, rubber dicks and industrial motors that littered the workspace. It was a veritable smorgasbord of fuck torture.

Walpurgisnacht turned back to Moira with a wicked smile and an orgy sized bottle of baby oil. He slowly started to flick the liquid over Moira's naked body like it was holy water.

"We want you nice and slick." The doctor continued to splash the oil. "It makes it so much easier to conduct the electrodes, for sure." He tipped the whole container upside down smothering her and the entire bench.

The doctor threw his hands all over Moira's firm flesh and started to knead the oil into every nook and cranny of Moira's incapacitated body. Bony fingers dipped and rubbed into all of her crevasse and the good doctor was becoming visibly aroused, judging by the tent he was pitching in his pants.

"Your body is so supple, so strong, but I will break it in ways you can't imagine," the doctor promised Moira.

"But we can't do it here, there are too many cameras, you might get in trouble." Rocket signalled to the cuffs and batted her lashes at the burly guard.

"I guess we can go behind the sheds," acquiesced the guard. "It's not like you're going anywhere now is it?"

He stooped with the key to the chains and freed Rocket from the floor. It was the first time in years Rocket staggered on her skates. Her legs tingled with pins and needles from being cramped on the wet floor.

The guard opened the containment cage and led poor Rocket around to the back of some supply sheds.

"Now you play nice," the guard warned, "or I'll open that little slut head up with this." He thrust the sub-machine gun into her face.

"Anything you say, big boy," cooed Rocket, "just get me out of this fucking weather."

He shoved her down on to her knees and unzipped. She scooped him up into her mouth and started to suck, all the while keeping a watchful eye on the barrel of the gun that hovered only inches from her face. Rocket could bide her time.

The guard started to moan as Rocket gulped down deeper and faster on his dick; with a free hand he encouraged her by forcing her head down on his prick, causing her to gag for a second.

The guard tipped his head back and let out a pleasurable moan. The gun moved a tiny bit to his right, just away from Rocket's face.

The moan of pleasure became a howl of confused agony as Rocket ripped her head away from his body with his member still in her mouth.

A massive pulse of blood emanated from his hips, spraying the girl in front of him in a wide fountain of red. The gun was out of his hand a second later, the butt of which Rocket used to crunch across the bridge of his nose. He went down like a sack of shit; the guard pissing his life out at an alarming rate.

Rocket was on him like a shot. Holding the gun to his head she straddled him. She ground her pussy on to the pumping wound in the guard's crotch and smiled a row of teeth slick with gore as she gobbed out his cock on to his chest. The guard whined as she took the severed member and started to stuff it into the dying man's mouth.

"Consider your back, scratched, you fucking mongoliod cunt!"

She rocked on where his dick used to be. His warmth flooded out of the guard and on to her pussy. Still grinning like a loon she squeezed the trigger and snuffed him out with a crack of gunfire. A splatter of brain matter splattered up the back of the shed.

Rocket tossed the gun aside. She stood up over what was left of the guard, gore running down between her legs. She had always seen murder as a form of art and this was truly one of her finest pieces yet.

"I think I should call this one..." She paused and cocked her head to contemplate the title of her latest work. *"Don't be a dick."*

The doctor looked up from between Moira's spread arse and smiled a deathly smile. He was holding what looked like two glass rolling pins. Cables ran from the batons to a large black box on the *toy* covered bench.

The tips of the glass rods were almost touching when an arch of electricity bolted between them. Walpurgisnacht giggled with excitement.

"I don't know what you want me to tell you 'La-La', I don't even know why I am here?" Moira tried not to let any fear creep into her voice but she was aware that she might have failed. The doctor raised an eyebrow and stopped smiling for a second.

"No, no, no," his head tilted to the side like a dog and an air of genuine concern sneaked into his voice, "You misunderstand me, love. I don't want you to talk, I want you to cum."

Chapter 6

Fire-Crotch was like a dog that hadn't seen its owner for the whole day. She couldn't stop jumping over Teapot when she entered the bar. She was a ball of fiery red haired excitement and relief but she still stank of piss and pussy. And Fire-Crotch looked like she had been hit by a car.

"I just know everything will be okay now that you're back, Mistress."

Teapot was flattered by both the confidence and the (hopefully) temporary promotion but had to show her stern side. If ever there was the time to crack the whip it was now.

"Control yourself, slut." The recruit jumped to attention. "Fix me a large Black Russian then go clean yourself up. You look like a fucking disgrace."

Fire-Crotch flung her arm up into a salute but let a little smile poke through. She jutted her breasts out and yapped, "Sir, yes sir!"

The rest of *Local 405 Roller Sluts* had turned out in full force. Mad Molly and Sally Blood-Fuck stood by the jukebox bopping their hips. They were slamming down shots and filling the machine with coin after coin.

Molly was the taller of the two. She was wrapped in biker leather, thick around the tits and hips. Her short, dark hair was liberally flecked with electric blue highlights. Molly had blood red war paint streaked under each eye.

Sally couldn't have been more different. She was a picture of a perfect 50's pinup. Her hair and nails *did,* dressed all up in polka-dot and tight black jeans. Ruby lips set her pale face. Her blond hair was done up in a bright red scarf. You just knew she had a flick-knife in her cute little clutch bag sitting and waiting next to her smokes.

There was no sign yet of 'The Gorilla'.

Thick Steve stood behind the bar, arms crossed as usual, tapping his huge foot to the tasty jams the girls had selected, but his eyes didn't leave the priest. It was something about the collar, that little white rectangle in a sea of black. It was as if it was some kind of pure light shining out. Thick Steve knew the priest's past. He was well aware of Father Billy's his reputation, he was no pure man. He probably had killed more men than all of them in the room combined.

He would watch him like a hawk; if he did anything to disrupt the family Steve would put him in the ground.

Meanwhile, Father Billy had lost the disguise and sat at a table on his own. He was cognizant of the daggers that Thick Steve was sending his way. Hell, he could almost feel them. Billy couldn't say the feeling was mutual; Thick Steve was a loyal dog to the girls. The bartender would drag his balls across broken, salt covered glass to protect them.

Father Billy approached the bar anyway. He could not tolerate Thick Steve's arrogant lack of respect for his elder. The bartender was just a drink-schlepper and he was *The Pimp Killer,* by god! Thick Steve needed a reminder of that fact. You know Father Billy has to fuck with him, right?

"Tell me," the priest began, "do you have any decent red wine back there, or is it all beer cans and cheap liquor?" The Priest fidgeted on the bar stool to get comfy. He was smiling in the Thick Steve's face just to get his back up.

"We might have some wine out back," Steve snarled and turned to search for the Priest's request.

"Thanks. Don't knock yourself out."

Steve trudged off. He acted as if Father Billy had asked him to wash the shit off of the underside of his car with his tongue.

Outside on the muddy drive up to the cabin, two low-riders pulled up slowly, headlights off. Thick smoke poured from the windows. The air was suddenly filled with the scent of weed and cheap cologne.

Teapot was drained; she flicked her boots off onto the floor and padded across the room to where Father Billy was waiting for his wine.

"I'm done for the day, might head back and crash, maybe join Fire-Crotch for a shower." Her tone was evocative but by no means an invitation.

The priest cleared his throat, his face a little flush. "You should rest. No point rushing in, not until we know what's going on." He placed a reassuring yet slightly sweaty hand on her shoulder. "We can start planning our next move in the morning."

The weary sergeant said nothing more and strutted off into the back rooms of the cabin. Steve slammed a bottle on the counter. "This is all we got!"

Father Billy scrutinised the dusty screw capped bottle, it was covered in cobwebs and the label faded. Something about *Vin De Gobblefuck* and *1995* was all he could make out.

"Well I guess that will do, my man. Don't suppose… " Steve turned with a huff and went back out to the store room leaving the priest with his hand in the air, midsentence, "… I could get a glass. Don't trouble yourself, I'll get it."

The priest pried himself off of his seat and walked around to the other side of the bar and searched for a clean glass. There was a selection on a shelf above the bar, but just as he reached up to fumble around he felt the cold of a shotgun barrel press against the back of his head.

Thick Steve had the jump on him. "Don't you ever come on my side of my bar, PRIEST!" he snarled.

How had he not heard the lump sneak up on him? Father Billy wondered. The big man certainly was light on his feet.

"I'm just getting myself a glass, Steve. No problem here, mate." A hard to swallow ball started to swell in his throat.

"Drink from the bottle like everyone else."

It was then that the front of house windows exploded in a hail of gunfire.

The Cheapside Pimp Collative stood shoulder to shoulder and raised their weapons. The sky was instantly lit up with bursts of muzzle flash. Round after round smashed into the front of the cabin as each man emptied their weapons. The *pop* of a grenade launcher ended the frenzy and the front of the cabin coughed out an explosion of fire and smoke.

Seconds later, all was quiet. The floor was littered with shell casings and the air filled with the egg smell of powder smoke. The Bunker's front porch was completely gone.

It was their leader, Running Wild that stepped forward with a megaphone in hand. His pink silk tracksuit rippling gently in the breeze, his matching trilby at a jaunty angle; his gold chains highly polished. He held up the megaphone to a mouthful of gold and diamonds.

"NOW… if any of you mother fuckers are still breathing in there…" the sound of his grill clicking in his mouth sounded like a tiny sword fight as he spoke. "You send out that one-eyed bitch, or we open up again until this shithole is a pile of sticks. You dig, niggaz?"

There was silence. Nothing could be heard except the tinkle of broken glass and the occasional spark from the now destroyed pink neon sign on the wall that used to say 'fuck off'. Then came a voice.

"Go fuck yourself, Wild!" Teapot's voice rang out. "You'll have to come get us, pussy!"

"Is that you Teapot, you fucking Cyclops?" The pimps started to reload. None of them were aware of the hulk walking up the drive. "Why don't you do you and your sluts a favour bitch, just come on out. We need to have a talk about what happened to my nigga, Sonny."

The first of the pimps was taken out silently. He was a straggler at the back, his neck snapping in a headlock like the bone of a chicken.

"Sonny deserved what he got." It was the priests turn to shout. "You and your crew are next on my list, Wild."

Two more pimps were dragged into the bushes, picked up like they weren't even there and shaken like wet towels until they both stopped moving.

"Hoo-ha, well, well, well niggaz. Is that Billy, The Pimp Killer's, big mouth I hear?"

Another two of Wild's crew had their heads slammed together with such force that their brains were mashed together into a grey matter smoothie. She rubbed the gore down her face like war paint.

"I'm glad you're alive, nigga, I wanted to take you out myself. I'm gonna mount your fucking head on my wall like an antelope or some shit."

The last of Wild's men was snapped over the woman's knee like a fucked pool cue and flopped to the ground like a sack of potatoes; still without making a single sound. Wild was too busy getting off on the sound of his own voice to notice that he was now on his own.

"Fuck you, Wild!" There was real anger in the priest's voice. "The day you take me down is the day hell freezes over, you cunt peddling piece of shit."

"Well if you're not coming out, then I suppose you leave me no choice." Running Wild's hand went up in the air like he was about to start a drag race. "OPEN FIRE, NIGGAZ!"

Nothing, not one round was fired; silence.

"What the fu..."

Wild turned around only to come face-to-tits with the biggest, blackest woman he had ever seen. No body-builder on earth could have been as big as the beast that stood before him. She was a mass of raised veins and tight muscle. Her tank top almost ripping off her frame as she swelled with anger and her shaven head glistened with sweat.

She snorted thick clouds of condensation and snot from her nostrils, her hands still bloody from killing Wild's men. She snarled at the pimp as he filled his pink silk tracksuit bottoms with the contents of his bladder.

"I'm going to fucking eat you... *NIGGA!*"

Chapter 7

The projector screen was tatty; old, barely hanging on to the roller and stained yellow with years of tobacco smoke and semen. The images being projected onto it were just as old.

A woman knelt in front of an aroused stallion, stroking its member into her mouth. Another woman, bound and gagged was brought out by men in black combat attire, it was clear that the struggling woman was there without her consent.

The two men chained her to a wooden fence and left.

The woman on her knees got up and led the randy horse over to where the bound woman was presented. Without hesitation the horse mounted her.

"This is just great Mayor, just us guys hanging out, watching a few stag movies together." The sweaty mass of lard that was Chief Lloyd Felchman was quivering with sexual excitement, a beer in one hand, the other rubbing the crotch of his trousers.

Mayor Rodney rolled his eyes. "For god sake Lloyd, settle down, it's only cocaine and a porno, not a fucking orgy."

The mayor turned to a huge pile of white powder on a silver platter and took a tea spoon to it. The substantial mound on the end of the spoon didn't stand a chance with the Mayor's greedy nose. It disappeared up into his head with one gigantic snort.

His hands came up to run his fingers through his silver hair, his eyes rolled up in his head. His gag reflex kicked in as a huge slug of the coke glugged into his gullet, numbing the nerves as it slid down the back of his throat.

His right canine tooth had gone completely numb and his dick had started to shrivel into his body. *God damn, did he ever love cocaine.*

"Can I have another bump, Mr Mayor?" The fat man's voice pulled him away slightly from his high. His eye's flickered open to see the chiefs bloated face, tongue hanging out and bagging like a big fat, pink hairless dog.

Reluctantly he dipped the spoon into the pile and dug out a small portion, nowhere near as substantial as the one he had just fed himself. The chief fell on it greedily, a little in one nostril, a little in the other.

The mayor was disgusted by the sight of the lump doing all his coke, he abhorred the man; it made him sick to the pit of his stomach. The sooner he could have him killed the better.

"One of these days you're gonna have to buy your own blow, you fat fuck."

There was a knock at the door, and both men jumped out of their skin. They were so high that they had forgotten about the outside world. Chief Lloyd looked like he was going to have a heart attack and the mayor reached into his desk for his concealed pistol.

The door opened and the blood in the men froze as a figure stepped into the darkened room. It was Dr. Lars Walpurgisnacht. Both men breathed a heavy sigh of relief. There was still something in the mayor's mind that made him want to shoot the doctor. He shook the thought off and extended the dust covered spoon.

The doctor waved it away. "Thank you kindly, but not until I finish my work." He walked around the desk with the mountain of narcotic on it. "I'm glad you're enjoying my cocaine."

"Your cocaine?" The mayor nearly choked. "What do you mean *your* cocaine?"

"Let me explain." The doctor sat in a chair in front of the two men and removed his wire framed glasses. "I had the drugs and the bodies of the gang members planted at that crime scene so I could hold the Mistress Moira in our cells until I could have her removed and taken to a location of my choosing." A smug grin crossed his thin lips.

Chief Lloyd's mouth hung open in astonishment, his hands shivering from the buzz of the high grade *crackle*.

The mayor put his hand back in the desk. His fingers poked around for the pistol.

"And now that I have her in the secret location I can move on with the next phase of my plan, for sure." With a snap of his fingers, four huge officers dressed in all black tactical gear burst into the room. Their machine guns were pointed in the faces of the stunned coke heads.

"Zip-tie them up and get them to my car… and one of you, bag up my drugs." The doctor stood up and crossed the room to leave. "Unfortunately gentlemen, the Mistress' little friend has managed to escape, but she won't get far. The little cunt has no clothes on."

Rocket had managed to throw herself from a wall onto the roof of a police truck. She was eyeing up some bushes as the large six-wheeled transport slowed for some traffic lights.

The light had gone to green. She made her move just as the driver slammed his foot on the gas sending the naked girl into a fast roll. Rocket landed awkwardly in the bushes, sending her arm way up behind her back, it had almost dislocated and the pain made her cry out: "CUNT!"

It was a dark night and the rain hadn't let up. She was still as naked as the day she was born and on the out skirts of the suburbs near the golf course. Rocket would have to find something to cover up with or get off the road. Maybe find her way into a house or…

The club house at the golf course.

There would be no one about at this time of night. The place was shut. Rocket deduced that there was bound to be a sports jacket or at least some goofy golfing trousers in there.

Rocket hopped over a short fence into a small wood that surrounded the course. She landed somewhere near the 13th hole. Rocket could see some flood lights in the distance, between the trees that edged the car park that lined the roof of the clubhouse. Fuck it if she was caught on the CCTV. Rocket wasn't planning on hanging around, just a quick in and out.

The soft floor of the woods was covered in all sorts of detritus. Wearing nothing but roller skates made the trek quite a chore for Rocket. She stumbled around holding on to whatever tree or shrub she could find to steady herself with.

The going was a little better when she got out into the open and on to the fairway; at least her wheels rotated, even on the grass. It was cut so short it looked like pool table cloth.

Rocket zipped over the giant green baize towards the backlit gothic looking building. It loomed over the course from its elevated position on the hill. She was expecting Vincent Price to be the door man when she approached the front of the old, evil looking building.

"This place gives me the fucking willies." She shuddered from a combination of cold and mild fright.

The service door around the side of the building that led to the kitchen was as easy to get into as a packet of bread. It was locked but with a slight nudge with the heel of her skate it popped right open.

Rocket scoured the kitchen for chef's whites. All she could find was an apron and chef's hat. She put those on and tied it up tight around her back, just above her firm arse. She tied the strings in a little bow. With the strings drawn tight, it just about held her ample bosom in place. Although if she tried any star-jumps she'd be spilling herself out all over the place.

With a wiggle of her hips she slid on the tall tube of white cloth and gave a little victory spin in the middle of the kitchen, but she couldn't hang her forever. She grabbed a long, wicked looking carving knife and headed on.

The solid resin wheels of her skates clicked as she rolled over the groves in the black and white tiles; through some double swing doors into a staff locker room. The room smelt of onions and disinfectant and was covered in glamour girl pin-ups.

None of the lockers had anything worth stealing in them until she spied a bag on the floor of the last locker. Great success. A pair of elasticated, checked chef's pants. They were huge and made her look like a clown but at least she wouldn't get arrested for indecent exposure… just breaking and entering.

…Oh yeah, and killing that cop.

Everyone's so fucking sensitive these days, thought Rocket.

Chapter 8

The front of the Bunker was shot to shit. All of the windows and the swing doors were gone and the wooden walls were riddled with holes. Pink and blue neon light from inside shone out into the dark of the forest.

Part of the porch had collapsed in the explosion and tables had flipped around like cardboard beer mats. The chairs had been splintered into matchwood. Carnage.

Outside, one of the local pimps was sounding off over a mega phone. He was barking orders and asking for the one-eyed bitch. As if that was going to happen any time soon.

Father Billy raised his head over the bar to sneak a peek at what was going on outside. Through the smoke he could see the skinny white boy in his pink track suit and hat shouting down the bull horn. What a waste of skin. He would have to make the pimp pay for what he had done, breaching the sanctity of the Bunker.

Father Billy could hear himself shout something back at the pimp but couldn't recall what it was. His head rang from the sudden grenade explosion. He stepped back and stumbled over something. It was what remained of Thick Steve.

Something was sticking out of Thick Steve's face. Some debris from the explosion stuck deep in the spot where his eyes and nose would have been. His hands were up, like a dead rat's and his fingers twitched as his brain's remaining electro functions fired for the last time. His tongue was wiggling out as the wound above his mouth oozed gore. Poor Steve, the thick son of a bitch.

The Father mumbled the last rites under his breath and waved his hand over the corpse with the sign of the cross. Steve would not allow god in his bar. Father Billy hoped that god would let Steve into his.

Billy checked to make sure his pistol was still in his pocket. Then he turned back to the angry pimp outside. His boys were loading up for another assault; this could be it.

But something else was happening out there. Running Wild couldn't see it, he was too busy grabbing his own dick and shouting at the building through the megaphone; but Father Billy could see it.

A huge black woman with a shaved head in a white tank top moved with savage speed through the men behind the skinny pimp. She was snapping and smashing them then tossing them aside like ragdolls.

It was The Gorilla.

She had been given that name in prison by some Nazi gang and she thrived on it; to be fair, she had killed every last member of that gang when they all got out, but she held the name dear. Now she was ripping the shit into the pimps outside.

All that remained was Running Wild.

Through the smoke Billy couldn't really see what was going on but he could certainly hear. Wild was screaming all the air from his lungs, something about "MY NUTS, PLEASE NOT MY NUTS!" before he slumped to the ground.

The Gorilla strode into the wreckage of the bar, blood smeared all over her face and hands as she chewed on something meaty.

"What up?" greeted The Gorilla.

The people carrier rolled through the suburbs, keeping a steady speed as to not draw any undue attention. The passengers were jammed in pretty tight. There were four heavily armed security personnel inside and one up front with the driver. Mayor Rodney and Chief Lloyd were zip-tied and gagged face to face on the floor.

One of the security men put his boot hard into the gut of the chief. Lloyd's eyes bulged and cheeks blew out as he vomited into his taped-up mouth.

"Look at this fat fuck. He makes one bust thirty years ago and he thinks he's the shit."

"Doesn't matter, he's in the deep stuff now. I don't think the doc is going to let the fucker walk from this. Did you see all the coke they had in there?" Another officer leaned in.

"Yeah man, and that fucking stack of old animal porno? What a couple of weirdoes."

A third man chimed in: "Good job we busted in when we did. I wouldn't want to catch these two fisting the shit out of each other, right?"

The guard in the front seat tuned round to get recognition from his bros. "Sick fucks," he commented. "They probably got kiddie porn on their computers, too."

The forth guard in the back rested his feet up on the mayor's head. "And this prick, tried to bring in a law to stop my kids from going to a local school near my house. If it had come in they would have had to take a bus for an hour to one of those *ethnic* schools." He gave the mayor a dig with his heel. "The prick!"

The driver piped up, "It's okay guys, when I was tidying up after their little wanking party I snagged a shit-ton of that blow." The car fell silent for a second. "What do you say, when we drop these dick heads off you wanna hit a few titty bars and get loaded?"

The car erupted in cheers and high fives. It was like a mobile frat house. The two men on the floor looked at each other in despair. They didn't like their chances.

"We better look alive, we're nearly there," The driver spoke again as the rest of the men composed themselves.

The car pulled into the gravel drive shrouded in the ominous gothic castle's shadow of the *Hambrook House* golf club.

The driver swung the car around the back to where two more guards waited by the cellar doors. The men jumped out, dragging the two bound men across the gravel and down the stone steps to the dark basement of the club house.

None of the men saw the half-naked female chef on roller skates watching them from the kitchen window. She ducked back down as the men reappeared and got back into the car.

"Now boys, let's get fucked up."

Father Billy sat in the wrecked Volvo. He was watching in his wing mirror Fire-Crotch rip everything out from the back of the car. He was still wondering how he was going to fit the Gorilla in there.

She came lumbering down the stairs. She moved differently to when she wasn't killing people, like a monster. The Gorilla was almost dragging her huge knuckles. She was the biggest person he had ever seen. To say she was ripped was an understatement.

"So you don't get mad when they call you the Gorilla, then?" All the girls stopped what they were doing and stared at the priest. Father Billy knew he was pushing her buttons but he needed to know where the line was.

"Nah, way I figure, I'm the biggest mother in this jungle; it's my fucking jungle." Even her smile had muscle tone.

"I don't know how we're going to squeeze you in this car, big girl," Father Billy wondered aloud. "Perhaps you could sit up on the roof?"

Her hand rolled into a fist the size of a bowling ball and she beat her chest twice with the hollow sound of a hammer hitting a barrel.

"I'm staying here," The Gorilla stated emphatically. "Now that Steve's dead the place needs a new owner." She whipped the keys from her back pocket and jiggled them in Billy's face. "It's okay Father, I'll keep the beer lights on for you and the girls." She stopped and looked at the priest. "But you best be looking after them, or you'll end up like them poor arseholes."

~GREGOR COLE~

Her massive hand waved to the pile of broken bodies Mad Molly was dousing with petrol and a dry lump formed in his throat. He knew that she meant every word.

The Gorilla smiled again and walked past Molly and Sally Blood Fuck. She smacked Sally on the arse as she walked by. It was like the sound of a branch snapping. The girl winced in pain almost dropping to one knee. But soon she was all smiles as she threw a match onto the stack of dead pimps. The pyre went up, instantly filling the air with heat and the smell of burning flesh and fuel.

"And these two bitches are staying to help me tidy up," ordered The Gorilla. "I'll need to add some extra muscle in case the pimp's boys show up looking for that piece of shit."

He wasn't going to argue with her. "Fine with me. We're going to see if we can't dig up anything on the Mistress' whereabouts."

"You guy's be careful, there's some strange shit going down." She hoisted up the little retro chick and carried her into the building on her shoulder. Sally squealed with delight and kicked her legs. Father Billy winked and nodded as the other two girls got into the clapped out car.

"You take care now, Gorilla." He shot her a sly smile, but she didn't turn to see it. She had her hands full.

Chapter 9

"Weed yeah; you want to buy some weed?"

The young couple coming out of the theatre scurried past the Rasta with the small baggies of pungent green in his left hand.

"Come along, Linda." The man pulled his girlfriend away as she paused for a second, like she was taking on board the notion of getting high. The pair waved down a cab in the wet street and gone.

"Your loss, this shit is dank, I tell you man." The Rasta turned to come face to face with Billy, The Pimp Killer.

His blood froze in his veins and his eyes locked with the man in the white collar for what seemed like an age.

"I need your help, Selwyn," spat the priest.

"Me no help you, not the help you need, me ain't saying nothing." The Huge dreadlocked fellow tried to turn away, but he was grabbed under the jaw and swept off of his feet and into an ally around the side of the theatre.

The priest threw the dealer through the side of a makeshift awning into some bins. Selwyn fell awkward and heavy, knocking all the wind from his lungs and twisting him up into a weird ball of limbs and dreads.

He flopped over, onto his back in the wet slurry of the bins. "I won't tell you anything, nothing you hear me, Pimp Killer!"

"This is not good news Selwyn, not good at all." He pulled his trusty .38 from under his coat. "I'm wondering if my friend here can make you change your mind."

The priest shoved the barrel of the gun into the Rasta's groin. He pulled a face like he was going to be sick and his hands came up to grab the weapon. He changed his mind when the priest smiled and pulled the hammer back.

"Now all I need is a location, that's all and I'll let you peddle you wares for one more night, no fuss."

"I know who you want and you know that I can't tell you. What he do to me much worse that what you got in store," The Rasta replied with an air of cockiness, like the idea of what Father Billy had in mind was nothing. He was laughing despite the fact there was a loaded pistol pressing against his junk. He looked down and then back up to Father Billy. "Go ahead, won't do you no good."

Father Billy pulled the gun across about a foot and rested it against the Rasta's knee, and without breaking eye contact pulled the trigger. The pistol coughed a blast of lead and smoke out through poor Selwyn's kneecap. The tall man went into shock. Before he could even scream Father Billy had the weapon in the Rasta's mouth.

The warm barrel tickled the gag reflex at the back of his throat. He exhaled still fresh powder smoke out of his nostrils. The Rasta's eyes filled with tears. He looked down at the bloody stump that used to be his leg. His foot was lying to one side under the flood of gore from the wound. He'd loved those trainers and now they are ruined.

"Tell me what I want to know or I open your head up like a water melon. Then I will go and find the next scum bag dealer and *ask* him." The gun pushed deeper. "YOU GET ME, CUNT?!"

The priest forced the gun into Selwyn's throat. He couldn't hold back the vomit as the gun thrust its way down his windpipe. The priest's hand was pretty much most of the way in the Rasta's mouth. Sick bubbled out from either side of Billy's fist and the Rasta's throat bobbed out as the priest applied more pressure.

"You're quite good at this, Selwyn, you know? Maybe when this is over we can get you a wooden leg and put you on the corner." The priest started to twist the gun inside Selwyn's neck. "Cheapside can't seem to get enough cock-suckers these days."

The large Rasta tried his best to shake his head. His nose was now oozing sick and snotty, his eyes rolling about in his head.

"Are you going to talk or are they going to have to surgically remove this gun from your gut?"

~GREGOR COLE~

Selwyn nodded the best he could with the weapon in him. He could feel the rings of cartilage in his throat ripping with even the slightest of movements.

"Good, I just want to see Shaky Dave." He pulled the gun out with a sloping sound and flicked free a wad of vomit and saliva from the end of the barrel. It hit the wall with a splat.

"So, where's he at?"

Moira was still bound.

They had moved her in the night. They wrapped her up like a mummy and stuffed her into a coffin. She'd felt the sensation of moving, of sliding about in the back of some vehicle. But now she was in a dark room, in some sort of dungeon.

The place stank of rotten meat and was hotter than a greenhouse in mid-summer. The sweat rolled from her body.

Moira was suspended, naked above the ground on a curved metal frame. Her legs were in full splits with her hands tied behind her back. From the way her head was feeling they had definitely drugged her. Every limb, joint and muscle screamed at her in agony.

Her mouth was stuffed with cotton and her head was held in place with a strange cage. It was clamped in position with a series of screws that went deep into her skin. She could feel them pressing and scraping against the thick bone of her skull as she tried to move.

Moira was as weak as she had ever been from the doctor's gruesome sexual torture but she could hold out just a little longer. Maybe.

From what she could see of it dungeon was a web of catacombs. The faint sound of dripping water could be heard and there was a dull light coming from down one of the corridors.

Then she heard the clopping of those familiar hard leather shoes. Dr Lars Walpurgisnacht was coming to see her again.

A strip light flickered on above her and the dark room flashed alive with brightness. The walls of the dungeon were thick grey stone blocks with no windows other than in the door to the corridor. A layer of what looked like algae clung to the stones lower down. In front of her there was a huge open drain that was sunk into the black stone floor and she knew now where the stink of rotting meat was coming from.

Something deep down in the drain gargled and splashed around in the sludge.

The algae seemed at its thickest nearer the hole; a maze of green stood out from the black. It flourished in the moisture and cracks of the hard stone.

The doctor stepped through the door and into the light of the dungeon; he was smiling that unnerving smile.

"Well, my beautiful one," the doctor began, "we did have some fun back at the station house now didn't we?" He stepped behind her and grabbed a handful of her left breast, his hand sliding over it from the gallons of sweat the titty produced. "I wanted to see how much you could take before the main event." He twisted her tit then slapped it away in disgust.

Moira watched him circle her again and again without saying a word. The hard heels of his shoes were making that now dreadful clip-clop noise on the stone floor.

"I wanted to make sure you had what it took." He laughed into his hand, never taking his eye away from hers. He wanted her to know that he was enjoying this.

The doctor stopped and turned to a white sheet that was covering another of his devices. Dramatically he threw back the cover to reveal his masterpiece. It was a huge diamond drilling rig with what could only be described as a three litre cola bottle of a dildo attached to it.

The doctor tugged at the sack barrow it was on and rolled it towards the bound Moira.

"I cannot wait to hear your screams with this working you over," he told her, "and then we shall start the summoning."

The doctor stuffed his hand in her mouth and pulled the cotton free, licking the sweat from her brow as he did so. His breath stank of Wiener schnitzel, beer and stewed cabbage. Moira spat rage into his face, thus sending the German back a few steps. His face had gone from smug to startle quicker than a Michael Schumacher lap. Moira's still got a little fight left in her.

"Bring it on Fritz," Moira yelled defiantly, "let's see what *you* got!"

Chapter 10

Rocket was hiding under a snooker table.

It was draped in a dust sheet but she could see the security guard's feet as he strode into the room via a small gap.

A crackle of static on the security guy's radio spoke. "So, is there anything up there?"

"Nah, I thought I heard something but must have just been that joint I smoked. This place sure is spooky." The guard spat onto the floor to clear his throat. "I'm on my way back down, out."

No sooner had the guard clipped his radio back into position on his stab vest, then Rocket's vicious looking carving knife slashed a thick line of red across the back of the guards knee, severing the tendons. He hit the floor hard, rolling in agony.

But before he could even get to his pistol the blade struck again. This time the knife's edge went deep into his left eye socket. Rocket pushed and pushed until the blade had stopped at the back wall of his skull. The guard's hands went into a spasm for only a second then they fell to his sides. He was done.

The blade took some effort to pull out. Rocket definitely broke his cheek putting her skate on his face to wiggle it free. She liked the way it crunched and went all squishy as his face caved in under her foot. She felt a warm tingle deep inside her sex.

The security guard at her feet was wearing the same uniform as the douchebags that had attacked Mistress Moira's. Rocket reasoned that perhaps she could get some info out of the next poor sucker that she could pounce on.

This place was a stink-hole of iniquity. And it was the last place Father Billy and Teapot wanted to be. They were in the very heart of the pimp ghetto on the far corner of cheap-side. Everywhere they looked there was some kind of sick act being carried out by a rough hooker in a shadowed doorway or a dank alleyway.

On every corner stood at least one pimp, sometimes several, all of them dripping with gold and covered in the best tracksuits that money could buy.

Fire-Crotch stared out of the window at the women plying their trade; strapped up in day-glow boob tubes, miniskirts and fake fur. A woman with a black eye simulated a blowjob at her as they passed. She returned in kind with a middle finger.

"Fucking skank."

The priest swung the car into a small yard around the side of a derelict building. In the corner there stood three bums around an oil drum fire. The three men passed a bottle around amongst themselves. They muttered under their breath at the arrival of the vehicle.

The two girls got out first and stretched by the side of the car. The bums took even more notice when the priest got out. One of the down and outs threw a shit stinking hand rolled cigarette into the fire and hurried up the building's fire escape.

"Well, looks like our arrival is going to be announced for us." Father Billy checked his pistol.

"And I thought they would at least throw rose petals for us to walk on," Fire-Crotch said sarcastically. She reached down for a piece of wood with a rusty nail jutting out of it.

Teapot raised an eyebrow at her choice of weapon. "Classy," she said.

"Fuck 'em," Fire-Crotch shrugged and walked over to where the two tramps stood. Her skates sunk into the soft mud of the waste ground, but she stayed up on her stoppers.

One of the bums stroked his groin with a filthy gloved hand while swigging from the bottle. He smiled a row of black pegs at her and growled. The filthy pervert stank of shit and a million cigarette butts. He didn't last too long.

"You've not got an invi…" the bum started. He stopped his thought when the wood bounced off the top of the bum's skull with a slap. The nail in the wood carved a deep gouge in the man's forehead. His eyes rolled up into his head and he slumped backward. Fire-Crotch relieved the bottle from the unconscious bum's hand before he could hit the ground.

To have let the bottle drop and shatter would have been an unforgivable act of alcohol abuse.

"Now, are you just going to stand there with your mouth open?" Rocket asked and took a hit from the bottle. The booze was cheap and burned on the way down. It dribbled out from the side of her mouth. She wiped the liquid away with the cuff of her overalls. "Or are you going to jog your dirty arse up there and get your buddies so we can get this started properly?"

The bum was almost in shock for a moment. He babbled with fear at the sight of the roller-slut. She was pretty much standing over him as he cowered.

The bum started off up the fire escape like a rat up a drain pipe. Some other men had already started to congregate in the battered up doorway at the top. They became agitated when the lookout arrived and explain what was going on at ground level.

The group of men started to cheer and growl as they made their way down the metal stairs. There was a rabble of dirty bodies almost fighting each other to get at the bitch that had taken out one of their brothers.

They stopped at the bottom of the fire escape to find her laughing her head off. The dumb bitch was standing there just pointing and laughing. The ring leader took a step forward as the rest of them hung back, sniggering and goading the girl.

"So, you want to play do you, little girl?" The tramp asked her. He then made a grab for Fire-Crotch's pointing hand but she was too nimble and darted behind the bin fire.

"Quick little bitch ain't ya?" He rubbed his dirty hands over his balding head. "But I'll get ya, I promise And when I do, me and my mates are going to have a party with you." The bum raised his voice and threw a look at the other two that had pulled up. "AND THAT GOES FOR YOUR FRIENDS, TOO!"

Teapot and Father Billy sat on the bonnet of the clapped-out motor. They shared a cigarette and watched as their girl had her fun. Rocket waved at the big tramp as he did his *hard-man* routine.

"You are such stupid fucks," Fire-Crotch judged. She patted the lump of wood in her hand, smiling at the lead bum. "If you *stinky* bastards took a bath and cleaned your *stinky* dicks every once in a while, you'd have noticed that you have petrol up to your ankles." She started to laugh like a fucked-up sideshow clown. There was a clang of resin roller skate wheel on the side of the burning oil drum.

The men at the bottom of the stairs could do nothing as they lit up like bonfire night with a *whoosh* as the air around them was sucked away by fire.

Their leader started to make a run for the roller-slut but was engulfed by the conflagrations before taking another step. His beard and ragged cloths went up in gorgeous flames. Soon he was running around the yard like a headless chicken that'd been set on fire. He was flapping his arms as black smoke belched off of him.

Fire-Crotched giggled and hopped with excitement as the night air was filled with the screams of burning tramps.

The pair by the car swanned over; Teapot put her hand on the young, enthusiastic assistant's shoulder and quietly spoke into her ear.

"As much as I love your style, and I do love your style," she brushed away a curl of red hair and licked her lips, "but how the fuck are we supposed to get up there now with a pile of burning bums in the way?"

The young redhead hadn't thought that far ahead. Rocket's bubble had well and truly burst.

Father Billy had wanted to step in as she was pouring the petrol over the bottom of the metal stairs but Teapot had stopped him with a knowing look of her one good eye.

Sergeant Teapot straightened her eye patch. She said: "I guess we're just going to have to take the hard route."

All three of them looked into the derelict building with a sense of dread. The light from the tramp fire cast moving shadows within the gloom. Sporadic bursts of manic laughter and the pop of breaking glass bottles bounced around in the bare concrete walls of the warehouse.

This was Junkie Town. Father Billy and the roller-sluts were outgunned and outmanned.

Chapter 11

His eyes stuttered open. His head felt like it had a split up the back and his brain was trying to squeeze its way out of it.

Agony.

Something that tasted like oxtail soup trickled down the side of his face and into the corner of his mouth. The taste was bitter and warm. He didn't know if he liked the *taste* or not. It took a while for him to register that it was his own blood.

Where was he? He pondered. *What was the last thing he could remember?* It was being bundled first into a car and then into some god awful basement dungeon. It was out in the country. He could recall the smell of the country; that smell of animal shit and wet vegetation.

Then he remembered; he was a prisoner. This was a dungeon and those bastards had shoved him in here.

Why had they shoved him in here, what had he done? Then he heard a moaning coming from the other side of the cell.

In the gloom he made out the shape of someone fat, someone moving, trying to roll over onto their side. The shape in the dark was having trouble breathing. In actual fact the poor fat fuck was wheezing like one of his lungs had collapsed following a rather hefty beating. That's right; they had beaten the both of them. That's why his memory was a little fuzzy.

The bastards had given them both a kicking. Fuck, it was all coming back to him now.

They were minding their own beeswax, doing some blow and watching a porno in his office. Then they burst in, that fucking doctor and his henchmen. Then they were thrown in a car and brought here where they kicked the holy hell out of them. That man over there wheezing and bleeding and positively dying is the Chief of Police. He himself was Mayor Rodney. He remembered.

The mayor's hands were cuffed behind his back and he was sprawled out on his side. He could barely move from the pain which ached and stabbed in whatever part he tried wriggle free.

The mayor struggled through the pain and did manage to wriggle up the wall until he was sitting up. The fat man in the other corner did fuck-all. The chief laid there still groaning in the darkness.

"Shut the fuck up you fat sack of shit." The mayor spat his blood from his mouth. "Somewhere down the line I'm sure this is your fault."

A thick wooden door stood between them and the outside world. Behind it the mayor could hear the sound of someone talking into a radio.

It most likely was one of the son of a bitch security men that had given them such a brutal drubbing. What he would give to have a moment alone with the prick. The shape he was in however, the mayor probably wouldn't put up too much of a fight.

Then he remembered something else. It remained just a glimpse, a memory that was tucked away in a little room in the back of his mind. He could have sworn that when they dragged them into the building there was a girl with her tits out at one of the windows. Yes, he did see her, he was sure of it. She had a chef's hat on and her tits were pressed against the glass, then the lights went out.

Pretty naked cooks running about the place; fuck, how hard had the security guy hit him? The mayor enquired.

~GREGOR COLE~

More radios crackled behind the door, followed by the jangle of keys and locks unlocking. The dank room was flooded with bright light and two huge guards stepped in.

"You better not touch me, you fuckers," threatened the mayor lamely.

The men just laughed at each other and shrugged. One of them grabbed the mayor by his collar and started to drag him out into the corridor. The mayor attempted a struggle, but his body was letting him down. The other guard dragged out the limp, fat-body chief.

If the mayor was only in half as bad a shape as the chief he was lucky. The fat chief's face had ballooned into a mass of bruised lumps. Both of his eyes had been kicked closed; resembling split cricket balls. The mayor almost felt a flicker of pity for the prick.

All of the security men covered their noses from the stench of the fat man's voided bowel. He was covered in every bodily fluid that a human could contain and the smell filled the corridor.

"We're going to have to hose that one down before the ceremony. He's covered in shit." One of the security guards gave him a small kick in the ribs to check if he was still alive. The fat man twitched and coughed back into life, for the moment.

"You there!" boomed a voice down the corridor, "Get those men cleaned up and on to the gurneys. The doctor will not be kept waiting."

The rest of the security team moaned and muttered at the supervisors request but dragged the men out into a courtyard in a hurry. They turned the attentions of a fire hose onto the filth covered men. The mayor worried the blasts might finish off the poor Chief of Police.

The two men had their clothing cut away from them. Then they were both unchained and strapped to two medical trolleys and wheeled back into the building.

It was now that Mayor Rodney saw the true extent of the fat man's injuries.

There wasn't a single inch of the chief that wasn't bruised. He had deep purple stains and mounds of distention all around his torso. Those are the tell-tale signs of internal bleeding. The fat man was not long for this world.

A squeaking from the gurney's wonky wheels echoed down the cold passageways. Two big breasted nurses checked on the prone men as the trolleys trundled into another dank room. There the doctor was waiting for them. He was rubbing his hands together as the sounds of heavy machinery and low, lazy orgasmic moans filled the room.

Mayor Rodney cocked his head to get a glimpse of a woman that was bound up with her legs in the splits. He saw that she was naked and sweating profusely; her head locked in a gruesome cage.

A huge black dildo on the end of what looked like a hydraulic pump pounded and spun inside of the tortured woman.

Doctor Lars clapped and giggled with joy to see the two men on the trollies. He took a black box from his pocket. It had a red dial on the side which he twisted maliciously with thumb and forefinger. An evil grin painted his face.

The fuck-machine kicked up a notch. The rubber dick started to slam in and out of the woman with furious strokes. Her moans turned into earth-shattering screams of painful ecstasy as a mammoth orgasm visibly ripped through her entire body.

"For sure; now the ritual can begin in earnest." The doctor buzzed like a school boy awaiting his first hand-job from the dirty school nurse.

There was a rumbling from below the floor. A guttural belch of foul air had flooded out from a huge drain hole in the floor and the doctor danced.

"She is on her way, this is good, this is good; call for the minions, we must start at once."

The room started to fill with people covered from head to toe in fine red robes, their faces covered with grotesque black masks. Each of the minions carried something: a candle, a long silver framed mirror, a decorative chest. Then there was one with a lovely pair of ornate, long scissors.

They filed in and lined up at either side of the trolleys. The nurses and security men made their leave. The mayor could see the back of a security guard's head through the small window in the now sealed door.

The doctor threw a leaver on the frame that held up the woman being fucked by the giant drill and the whole contraption swung back horizontally. He then swung the rig closer to the drain. There was another rumble from within the drain followed immediately by a gruesome sucking sound.

The doctor fairly leaped over to the minion holding the scissors. He snatched up the dangerous looking cutters, and then bounced back to the centre of the room.

"She is coming, she is coming and she brings a new age to Cheapside" With another flick of his thumb he turned the fuck-machine up to full with the little black device and held up the scissors for all to see.

"The Queen will bring death and turmoil to all that oppose us. This is the dawn for the new way, my way!"

With the sound of the machine fucking the bound woman into oblivion he took the mayor's flaccid penis into his free hand and scooped at it with the sharp blades.

The mayor felt a devastating pinch as the blades snipped shut. At first it was like nothing had happened. But then there was this huge pulse of blood that had squirted out from the groin like Lucifer's drinking fountain.

Red splashed up the white coat of the doctor and across the floor towards the open drain. Dr Walpurgisnacht screamed with delight. The minions all about the room had started to chant in a low doom-like drone. The doctor swooped down a second time. This instance it was on the fat man's poor, unprotected genitals. He sliced them off as easily as he had the mayor's.

With bloody scissors raised above his head the doctor presented the two severed dicks over the open manhole. The rumbling within intensified. The strip-light overhead burst in a shower of sparks. The room was engulfed in a foul smelling wind from the pit below.

The doctor shrieked in triumph. "SHE IS HERE!"

Chapter 12

Fire-Crotch was still fighting on in the ruins of the deserted warehouse. Over the heavy breathing and mumbling of the junky mob the 'thwack' sounds of wood hitting skull could be heard.

From every nook and cranny junkies poured into the deserted building.

Dirty face upon dirty face, they started to swarm in a mass of shit stinking tramps and beat-up meth whores. Each of the skanks and bums brandished some kind of weapon; a broken bottle, a rusty knife, a length of pipe or wood. Things were not looking good.

Everywhere they turned there was another smack-head blocking their path; they were outnumbered and outgunned. Teapot help up her bloody fists and the priest held out the spent pistol on his finger only for the weapon to be snapped up by greedy junkie claws. The surge of bums proved too much even for her and there was a short scream and the sounds of a tussle close by.

Soon the circling tramps parted and Fire-Crotch's limp frame was dragged to her friend's feet by two of the disgusting creatures. She let out a whimper as they dumped her hard to the ground.

Teapot fell to her knees to comfort her dented assistant. She stroked her flame-red hair. A small line of blood streaked her hand and her good eye shot up and froze the first bum that made contact with it. Teapot was way past angry.

Father Billy tried to connect with the rabble, "We didn't want violence but you turned on us." Both of his hands were in the air as he stepped past the two girls on the floor. "All we wanted to do was find Shaky Dave."

"And what we're you expecting to do when you found him?" A voice boomed from behind the pack of junkies. It was a deep and powerful voice that seemed to jump from wall to wall as it echoed through the skeletal building.

"We came only for some information, nothing more," The priest voice trembled slightly, "but you moved on us first." He knew full well that if the junkies smelt even a fraction of fear they were done for.

"And I guess burning up a few of the brothers was us making the first move." The voice bellowed again. This time it sounded like it was behind them.

"You know it wasn't like that. If she had done nothing the girl would have been killed, or worse."

A tall shape moved around the circle of bums. The jingling of tiny bells sounded clearly with every step. The jingling drew closer as he started to shoulder his way through the pack. Thick white smoke poured from the shadowy figure like the funnel of a steam train. The figure hummed a deep, catchy tune.

Milky-white eyes peered through the darkness at the three intruders. A smile filled with silver teeth made Teapot nervous.

Shaky Dave stood before them, his dreadlocks tied up in a tie-dye linen bag that sat on his shoulders like a rucksack. "But you still burnt up my brethren." The rest of his long frame was rapped from head to toe in camouflage fatigues and hundreds of wooden bangles and pendants. "Burned them up real good, you did. Extra crispy."

"Let's just settle down now, let's not do anything too hasty, we just want a location of our lost friend and we're gone." Father Billy was determined to walk out of the predicament. It would be ungodly for the skinned body of a priest to be found in a crack den. What would his flock think? Besides, Father Billy wasn't ready to die just yet.

"You still want information when our brothers lay sizzling out in the rain? You got some nerve, Priest." Shaky Dave pulled a mean looking cleaver from behind him that looked like someone had just sharpened on side of a sheet of scrap metal.

He slid the blade close up the Adam's apple of the priest. Tiny flecks of stubble pinged off the blade as it glided over his skin.

A bead of sweat ran down Father Billy's temple. He tried not to swallow at the dust ball that was growing in his throat.

"Wait! Just think about this for a second." Father Billy used his best *plead for your life* voice. It was a voice he had heard from others many times. "Who is it that lets you have this place, lets you run Cheapside the only way you want?"

"What you mean, man?" Dave eased the lump of metal off a little.

"Mistress Moira."

The gang of junkies became still for a while and Shaky Dave turned to get a reaction from his brethren. All he got back was a bunch of dilated pupils and puzzled faces.

"What about the Mistress?"

"She's the one that lets you all get away with murder down here. And you know damn well that without her you lot would have been flushed out by every other gang out there. You owe her and you know it."

Shaky Dave nodded slowly in agreement and a smile crossed his lips. "That's true enough, man. You got thirty seconds to further convince me or I'll have to peel your fool head back."

With sweat dripping off of his forehead the priest felt as the pressure eased up a touch; for thirty seconds at least.

"She was taken by the police but a special security team planted drugs and dead bodies around the place."

"And you want me to what, help you find her?" Dave paced back and forth in front of the priest, turning the giant ghetto-clever to catch the dim light in the warehouse.

"If she dies this place will be fair game. First the pimps will come, then the skin-heads, then the bikers. How long do you think you and your junkies can hold out against that for?"

The camo-clad Rasta scratched at the back of his head under the bag of dreads. "You make for a good augment, and I know a way to find her, just need you to help me, holy man."

Father Billy didn't like the sinister tone in Dave's voice. And as the old saying goes, never trust a fucking junkie.

Shaky Dave signalled for his pack to disperse. As quickly as they had surrounded them they were gone. Back they all went: back into the cracks in the walls and under the piles of junk from whence they scurried.

Soon the air was thick with the scent of crack smoke and the sound of liquid bubbling up in dirty spoons as Dave led them up to his makeshift Temple on the top floor.

The room was draped in coloured cloths and patterned throws. Tiny silver bells hung on strings running from every corner. The whole room chimed and shimmered as a breeze streamed unimpeded through glassless windows.

In the centre of the room was a stone alter. It was littered with all sorts of dark paraphernalia. There were bones, chicken feet, jars filled with things that squirmed, peacock feathers and a selection of home-made knives as gnarly as Dave's botch-job cleaver. There were rolls of money, bowls of black liquid that had the acrid scent of cheap alcohol. A picture of a woman and her family lay on the altar next to a selection of wooden dolls, each one adorned with a lock of hair tied around their necks.

Teapot was the first to investigate the bizarre artefacts on display. She quickly realised that the dolls represented the woman in the photo and her three children. She flicked the hair that was wrapped around one of the dolls she held. It smelt of citrus oil. She threw it back onto the cold, grey stone surface. *Shaky Dave couldn't be as cold as to curse a family, could he?*

Fire-Crotch was just about coming around when Dave burst through a wall of coloured silk from a back room dressed in a leopard hide cloak holding a rain stick. He had lost the camo and was swinging free. His slowly engorging member was bobbing in front of his hips to the disco-throbbing beat of his pulse. Fire-crotch couldn't help but rub her eyes. *Was she still dreaming?*

"The redhead and the one-eyed bitch have to leave, but you stay Father." Shaky Dave started to shake the rain stick. It was accompanied by a flash of lightning outside that lit up the derelict building.

"I'm going to need your help, Mr Pimp Killer. We've got work to do!"

Chapter 13

The long red robe was itchy and she could barely see out of it. The robe smelt like it hadn't been washed since the last orgy it was most definitely used for.

Rocket wanted to scratch her arse from the itch of the fabric, but the candelabra that she was holding was too heavy to manage with just the one hand.

She shuffled along with the rest of the parade of itchy acolytes on the toe stoppers of her skates. Her hood was covering her face so that she could only see the floor. The last thing she needed was to hook the bottom of her robe to reveal a naked chef on skates.

The douchebag she had taken the robe from cried like a baby. Her carving knife rested pressed up as it was against his left testicle. She had beaten him, just a little bit, and then she stuffed him in a locker where he was getting changed. He wouldn't make a sound in there. Not while tied up with a ripped shirt. His own spunk-stained pants were stuffed in his mouth.

A low, orgasmic moaning could be heard as the procession shuffled into a boiling hot room. The moaning was twined with the sounds of vibrating machinery. A man with a thick German accent was cheering and laughing. Someone nearby was getting their leather thoroughly stretched.

From what Rocket could see, the stone floor was covered in some kind of bright green mould that had sprouted wholesale out from its cracks. The air was thick and warm with the stench of vaginal fluid and blocked drains. The buzzing became louder as did the cries of pleasure. Rocket felt a little left out. She tipped her head a little to try and snatch a glimpse of snatch.

She managed only to sneak a peek at a sweaty foot with black painted nails quivering and the back of someone's head. The hood of the robe obscured everything else.

~GREGOR COLE~

Rocket recognised the foot to be Mistress Moira's. After all, she'd been made to suck those toes a hundred times. She had painted those nails herself, the perks of being a sex slave.

Rocket knew she couldn't jump to her mistress's aid just yet. She may have been armed but she wasn't stupid. The security would've chopped her ass down in a hummingbird's heartbeat. No, she would see how it played out.

The squeaking wheels of trollies being brought into the room broke up the antics of the leaping German for a moment. Rocket felt a hand on her shoulder. It pulled her back out of the way. She nearly stumbled as her legs buckled slightly, trying to keep her balance on the rubber toe stoppers of her skates.

There was a slicing, clipping sound and the muffled screams of a man. Then there was some more slicing and snipping. The rest of the robed minions started to chant something that Rocket couldn't understand. They began to sway.

A rush of foul smelling wind came up from the floor. There was a flash of electricity and a popping sound as the strip light above them burst. The German became over excited, repeating over and over "SHE IS COMING, SHE IS COMING!" Rocket took a guess that he didn't mean the woman being fucked. Something was coming for Moira.

The wind started to pick up in and around the top floor of the derelict warehouse as Shaky Dave started the ritual. His huge dick had become fully erect as he danced around the stone altar; waving the rain stick around his head like a samurai sword.

"The women must leave." Teapot and Fire-Crotch looked at each other. Both of their noses were firmly out of joint.

"Why's that, may I ask?" Fire-Crotch barked at the naked Rasta.

"So you can get in a car and keep a phone handy. And when I find your mistress I will give you the location. I'm guessing it'll be somewhere way out in the sticks." The girls looked at each other. They both knew it was a good plan. "Time to get going, bitches. *Vamoose!*"

The pair nodded. Reluctantly they made their way down through the building to the clapped-out old Volvo. Teapot couldn't help but look to the roof of the warehouse as they pulled away.

Meanwhile, on the top floor of the warehouse, Father Billy stood in the middle of the room. He was holding himself a shovel. If he became taken by any of the more violent spirits he might call up, the priest was under the strictest instructions to hit the shaman with it.

The Pimp Killer, or no, Father Billy was not looking forward to it.

Shaky Dave took a handful of the black liquid from one of the bowls on the altar. He threw it at Father Billy, catching him full in the chest. The goo splashed up to his face.

The thick substance was warm but didn't feel wet in any way. It dried into his exposed skin as quickly as it has splashed onto it.

"What is this shit?" The priest asked. He couldn't hide his anger at the Shaman's actions.

"It will keep you safe from the spirits that might want to enter you. Believe me; you don't want to be fucked up the arse by some of these bad men."

Dave slapped his face with another handful of the black goo and returned to shaking the rain stick around the stone platform. Various junkie disciples cowered in the shadows, holding strips of piss stained cloth with black symbols scrawled on them, shaking them in time with the rhythm of the rain stick.

One of the junkies scurried out from under the altar with a wooden bucket, the bottom of which was thick soot. The scumbag dumped it on the table, flipping it over and pouring some of the black liquid onto it. Then he scuttled himself off into the shadows. It was time to light up his crack pipe and enjoy the show.

One must take time to smell the roses...

As if he was pulling it from his arse, Dave held aloft a burning torch. Its flame roaring as the storm inside the building started to rise. Coloured cloth and elephant bells whipped up and chimed as the winds tore through the skeleton of the derelict warehouse. A twisting cyclone of debris and incense smoke started to roll around the room. The men stood their ground, attempting in vain to shield their faces from all the flying objects.

Father Billy was getting battered by the bits of crap in their self-contained typhoon. A clay pot clipped and shattered off of the side of his head but he held firm and stood tall. Through the gap in his hands he could see Dave light the upturned bucket with the torch, Father Billy looked down at the black stain on his clothes and skin and wondered how flammable he had become. He looked back to the shaman. Dave's ever-hardening penis looked as if it was growing even bigger. It started to resemble an arm that was engaged with lifting something heavy. Said cock was thick and vascular.

Dave slammed down the rain stick onto the altar. It was accompanied by another flash of lightning that lit the room blue and a huge rumble of thunder slammed overhead.

"And now we see what they want hidden." Dave's body swelled with power and his dick looked like it would burst as he raised his hands to the sky. "NOW WE SEE WHAT THEY WANT HIDDEN!"

The storm raged on. Dave stood in the dead centre of the cyclone as it ripped the dread bag from his head. His locks flew around his head like crazy snakes. More flashes of electricity from outside as hundreds of small balls of electricity burst all around the city like fireworks as the tall man worked his magic.

Shaky Dave's voice boomed loud over the chaos swirling within the derelict building, "GIVE ME SIGHT TO FIND THE ONE THEY CALL THE MISTRESS!" he extoled. Dave grabbed the flaming bucket in time with another clap of thunder overhead. He held it up as if to show it to the monstrous god that was controlling the storm.

"LET ME SEE!"

Shaky Dave looked up into a faraway light that was deep within the dark space of the bucket. His eyes darted from side to side like he was reading the illumination.

"Mistress Moira is in the basement of the golf course clubhouse; the Hambrook House." He tilted his head to get a better look into the bucket. "There's something else, something evil. I need to get closer."

Father Billy typed a message on his phone to the girls in the old banger, using the spade to protect his head from more of the still swirling ceramics. The shaman's dreadlocks fell still at his back for a second as there was a lull in the indoor tempest. The priest looked around bewildered at the Rasta as he stood tall, staring into the bucket. He appeared to be in a profound trance.

Shaky Dave slammed the burning bucket onto his head. There came a big, pussy-fat surge of energy that sent Father Billy off his feet and across the room. He landed heavily on a pile of rubbish bags and junkies. Looking up he saw a blinding light emitting from deep within the bucket. Shaky Dave was screaming.

Chapter 14

Long bony fingers covered in gelatinous skin the colour of rotten pork slid from the darkness of the drain hole. They pushed their way into the gloom of the candle lit room. The stench coming up from the hole was almost unbearable but the doctor didn't care, this was his crowning achievement.

A row of black barbed horns poked out next; each wicked looking and covered with tiny hooks and points. They were sharp enough to cut human flesh at a glance. The doctor had studied and worked his entire life for this moment, the summoning of the Queen of Shit herself, Holzaarth.

Her head emerged from the drain like a thorny, slime covered turd being squeezed out into the world from the earth's arsehole. Its pug face was slickened with foul ooze. Its eyes darted quickly from side to side to get a bearing on its surroundings.

The demon flopped on to the floor like a wet fish and shuddered with the first intake of breath. To announce her arrival, it gave out a whining scream like a new-born.

"She is here, behold her beauty." The doctor danced around the room then pounced on Moira. Her eyes had rolled all the way up into her skull as another orgasm from the fuck machine rattled through her spent body.

The monster resembled a flap of rotten skin covered in twitching black spines. It looked like a week-old pig's ear that dog had chewed on. A see-through pink sleeping bag filled with shit and blood with spindly arms that whipped around as it righted itself like a new born fowl.

"The queen must eat. She has been sleeping such a very long time," Dr. Walpurgisnacht replied. He ripped the machine from between Moira's legs. The huge rubber fist-like dildo slid out of her slick hole with a popping sound. But something else followed it: a *light.*

There was a bright light emanating from her pussy. It was only just small one at first, but then it started to expand the mistress' shit wide open like she was on the verge of giving birth.

Queen Holzaarth clawed her way up the framed offering of Moira to witness the light and to take her first bite of human pussy. The beast's face was a mass of twitching sores and razor-like fangs. Its bloodshot yellow eyes blinked as the light from Moira's broken hole got brighter and brighter.

Something was coming through forcing its way into the world from deep within Moira.

What looked like slime-encrusted tentacles had started to whip their way into the world from the opening between the dominatrix's legs. This was soon followed by the head of a screaming Rastafarian.

Everything in the room went still for a second and all that were witness were agog with disbelief. Rocket could hold her patience no longer and threw back the hood of her itchy red robe.

"What the fuck's going on, you fucking fucks?"

The question broke the stillness of everything in the room. Rocket then realised that she was being stared at by a mad scientist, a horned demon shit queen and a trussed up dominatrix giving birth to a screaming Rasta.

"Shit!"

She recognised the head jutting from the pussy as the shaman from the junkie hovels in Cheapside. The head started to shout: "I HAVE FOUND THEM, FATHER BILLY! I HAVE FOUND THEM!"

The doctor flapped his arms and screamed at the security guards standing mute and stupid at the back of the chamber. "What are you waiting for, kill the bastard!"

The two security men looked at each other and shrugged. One spoke, "Fuck you, we quit." They turned, opened the door and left swiftly followed by the rest of the robed acolytes and the two busty nurses.

The Queen became enraged and rode back on her flap of a tail and with great swipes of her bony claws, slashed at the

Rastafarian's face. Lumps of skin and flesh tore away and blood sprayed against the walls with every swipe.

"This whore is a conduit between two places; I must sever the connection to close the channel." The doctor snatched up his scissors and darted for the exposed neck of the oblivious Moira. "The Queen must feast even if it is dead flesh."

A spurt of red emitted from the soft neck of the prone woman as the doctor's weapon parted flesh and opened vein. The doctor howled with delight as he pushed deeper and deeper into the wound until he hit the hard bone of her spine.

The light from her crammed vagina blinked around the bloody stump of a head a few times, and then it went out for good. The pussy instantly closed up around the neck of the mauled Rasta. His eyes popped out from their sockets from the sudden pressure. There was a snapping sound then a slop as all the gore from his head poured over the now dead woman's crotch. The head hit the floor with a thud.

"Seriously, what the fuck is going on?" asked Rocket. She was on the verge of a breakdown but still had the wits about her to raise the pistol. Rocket fired four shots into the back of the Queen of Shit's oversized head. A flood of shit and brain; the doctor looked to be in complete shock. He was just staring at the girl with the gun.

Then door to the cell burst open.

Father Billy swung the shovel. He hit the naked shaman in the back with a deep thump. The force of the strike sent the priest flying through the air with the greatest of ease.

The storm stopped suddenly. It was as if someone had flipped a switch. The light from the bucket had flashed three times, and then it died in a last, bright burst. That was then followed by a torrent of blood that flooded to the concrete floor.

Shaky Dave's arms fell to his side. He swayed hither and yon for a moment then fell back onto the hard ground with a slap. The bucket bounced away to reveal that his head was gone. There was nothing left but a gaping wound in the centre of his shoulders.

Father Billy sat absolutely still for what seemed like an eon to make sure his head wasn't the next item to disappear. Slowly his hands came up to rub away the blood from his eyes caused from the flying clay pot. He was relieved to find that his head still where it was meant to be.

A few of the junkies made for the exit, rats abandoning a sinking ship but one came over to inspect the burning bucket and his dead leader. He kicked the bucket across the floor, double checking that it was empty.

"Yep, he's dead alright."

"Thank fuck for that. That fucking guy was a huge pain in the ass," another voice from the shadows added, "Always shaking that ridiculous fucking stick, he was." A pile of trash stood up and shook off the debris from the storm. "And all that voodoo bollocks, I guess this is what happens when you mess with the dark arts."

The first junkie turned to Father Billy and waved him over. "You wanna kick this son of a bitch with us for a bit?" he queried, "maybe get real fuckin' high?"

Father Billy got to his feet, still in a daze from what he had just witnessed. He staggered over saying: "I'll pass if it's all the same with you." Then he remembered the text. He had sent Teapot and her bitch to the place where Shaky Dave's head now rested. The look of shock was still plainly visible.

But before he could turn to leave he found himself once again surrounded by the homeless. He could smell them all. They smelled sharp and dreadful; a bad penny. Each one looked down at their dead boss then looked up at the priest that had helped with his demise. Father Billy felt uncomfortable.

"I guess we are going to have to appoint another leader." The first junkie said and then he extended his hand in a gesture of truce. "I guess you'll have to do, Father, unless you have a better idea?"

As the rest of the junkies closed in, Father Billy knew that he didn't really have a choice.

He said to them: "For a while at least, I suppose I could steer you in the right direction, yeah?" He gipped the filthy hand of the head junkie and nodded reluctantly.

The crowd of bums joyfully erupted around him; high fiving and bumping fists. The priest was mobbed by ecstatic crack heads all wanting to slap the back of their new boss.

Billy was lifted into the air and a small glass pipe was shoved into his mouth. He had no choice but to draw on it. *When in Rome, he thought with a smile.* The thick smoke filled his lungs with heat and a wash of calm splashed over him. His head went a little bubbly and started to tingle. The rabble cheered as Shaky Dave's headless corpse was trampled under a surge of dirty trainers and black feet.

"ALL HAIL THE PIMP KILLER!"

Chapter 15

Teapot and Fire-Crotch burst through the door to the cell and ran straight into a blood bath.

The floor and walls were covered with blood, green mould and shit. What looked like a giant pile of melted pink plastic covering a thorn bush sat as a monument to bad art, right there in the middle of the floor. It was leaking faeces in wet, gargling coughs.

Moira's corpse was trussed up like a festive turkey on a frame. Her throat had been cut so deep that her tongue actually flapped through the wound like a cyanotic-blue flesh comma.

The ripped-up head of Shaky Dave the Junkie Lord was still rolling around on the ground at the feet of a dark haired man in a lab coat that was swathed in every body fluid conceivable.

And there stood Rocket. She was proud and topless, pointing a pistol at the face of the man in the lab coat. Fire-Crotch morphed back into *excited-dog mode* and dived all over her partner in crime. She slathered her in kisses and was squeezing every part of her firm body. Fire-Crotch slinked around her like a ferret eventually resting at her feet. Fire-Crotch's face was pressed firmly into the sweaty groin of the oversized chef pants.

Fire-Crotch breathed deeply of her counterparts scent. Rocket hadn't even twitched. The barrel of the pistol was still-dead bang between the doctor's eyes from across the room.

As Teapot scanned the body of her mistress, a sick feeling rose up from her stomach. She looked at the man in the lab coat with venom and yelled: "End that prick!"

The pistol spat one last round into the face of the twisted doctor, splitting his skull like a hot knife through butter. This evil brail splattered against the back wall. The doctor shook for a moment as his eyes rolled up to look at the hole in his forehead then slumped to the ground in a heap. His body flopped on top of his fallen Queen; the sack of rot let out a wet fart through its open head wound as the doctor's weight flattened out across it.

~VENGEANCE OF THE VIGILANTE ROLLER SLUTS~

Fire-Crotch flinched at the shot then squealed with delight to see the man's face cave in. She wiggled against Rocket's legs. Both of the girls magnificently fought off the urge to touch-fuck though Fire-Crotch's hand slid up Rocket's slender leg and found a resting place in the warm crack of her arse. In kind Rocket pushed out her firm butt. She was a good girl like that.

Teapot crossed the room and stood over the body of the good doctor. She raised her boot and brought it down hard on his jaw; it crumpled under the blow like a chicken bone.

"Bitches," she clapped her hands twice to snap the roller girls out of their blood lust. "Help me cut the mistress down. She will have a proper funeral."

The girls set about untying their fallen comrade as Teapot picked the mashed face from the heel of her jack boot. She had no idea what had happened here, or what had happened back at the derelict warehouse to warrant Shaky Dave's head to be chopped off. Teapot didn't want to know. All she knew for sure was that she was now in charge. The squad was hers to command.

It was a *battlefield* promotion, but a promotion, nonetheless. And a battlefield it will undoubtedly be.

Without Moira in charge, there's going to be a void, with the streets being seen by many as up for grabs. Not everyone will accept Teapot beyond her Sluts.

~GREGOR COLE~

From Cheapside to the Suburbs, war was coming and it would be wearing a cheap gold tracksuit. Every pimp and pusher would now attempt to stake a claim and it was down to her now to see them off.

Something under Teapot's eye-patch itched.

Teapot buckled her storm-trooper's helmet under her chin and sucked back the tears she was saving for this very event. She would grieve, but not in front of any underling bitches.

"We're leaving, back to The Bunker," she said. Then Teapot turned and left the cell shouting over her shoulder, "And Rocket. Stay naked bitch!"

Teapot had started the beat-up old Volvo while Rocket and Fire-Crotch had wheeled out on their skates. They were carrying the lifeless body of Moira between them like a stretcher.

Carefully they placed her in the back of the estate car, laid out and driven slowly like a state funeral. The drive back to The Bunker was quiet, sombre even. Not one of the girls said a word.

They were making their way through every part of Cheapside to display the body, everyone would know by the time they got to The Bunker.

The bells of St. Dennis sounded like never before. They chimed a death knell for the fallen Mistress of Cheapside. The congregation had swelled in numbers and filed up the vast steps to the ominous door of the chapel.

All the street scum had come to pay their respects; the inside of the church was like a furnace with the amount of candles lit. Junkies and pimps lined the pews, side by side in a single moment of solidarity, a moment of peace before the oncoming storm of war.

Father Billy had dressed in his usual cassock but with one of the junkies scrawled sheets of dirty rag around his neck to signify ownership of the warehouse drug den.

He was now a king of Cheapside, a keeper of the peace.

"Let us not forget that this woman was a warrior. She died a martyr in a way of such depravity it will remain unmentioned in the house of god." His voice echoing around the massive hall, "let us take a day to grieve, time to reflect what this woman brought, calm harmony and order within the houses." Murmurs of recognition swept over his newfound flock.

"She died at the hands of people that would destroy us. Whose desire is to bring about a new evil to the streets of Cheapside."

Some of his junkies had started to hit the pipe in the back, some had fallen asleep under the pews; others were fighting over drink.

"But know this dear friends, brothers and sisters," Father Billy raised his hands to quieten the crowd, "anyone that fucks with my flock will die like a dog!"

The congregation erupted.

The Gorilla was sweeping up at the front of The Bunker when the car pulled up. She had heard the news and got the other girls to build a ceremonial bonfire for the body out front where they had burned those wretched pimps.

Teapot got out and jogged up the steps. She buried herself in the huge embrace of the bruiser. She tried to hold back the tears but there was such a safe feeling in the arms of the giant that she couldn't help but let go.

"It's okay baby girl; Gorillas got ya." The beastly woman rocked her gently. "Now you go in back and clean up. We can take care of what needs to be done out here."

Rocket and Fire-Crotch dealt with Moira's body. As Teapot entered the bar, a couple of contractors were busy rebuilding the front porch. They nudged each other with their elbows as she passed.

"Hay girl, if you shift that eye patch I don't mind skull-fucking ya." The builders laughed and continued nudging each other. Teapot stopped in her tracks and cocked her head in the direction of the workmen.

The builders caught a glimpse of pure fucking fury in her good eye and stopped laughing. It was a look that could freeze marrow in the bone, a look that could castrate at a hundred yards. They hurried back to work.

The shower was hot and Teapot washed away the filth of a torrid day. She towelled herself down and strapped herself into some fresh military fatigues and a corset. The Gorilla had put out her best commissars hat and leather gloves. A new riding crop sat on top of a wicker basket; it was tied up with a neat pink ribbon with a tiny tag hanging off it with a single word written in black marker, 'Mistress!'

A broad smile crossed her face and she stepped out into the bar to face her new troops. If war was coming they would have to prepare, and quickly.

Teapot strutted across the room, and just as the builder with the big mouth looked up to say something witty about her hat, she swiped the riding crop across his face. A huge red welt rose up instantly and he fell back into a pile of splintered wood panels.

Stepping over him she put her jack boot on his chest and bent over, her face in his. "I'm going to break you first and you're going to thank me, fucking worm." The workman could only manage a mumbled dribble as he nodded his head like he was in spasm his mate looked on in disbelief.

Teapot stepped out into the yard where the body of the last Mistress was starting to burn atop the pyre the girls had built. Her troops stood front and centre, looking up at their new leader backlit by fire and black smoke.

A rumble of a 450 engine up the gravel road could be heard as Father Billy pulled in on Teapot's trusty bike. He was wearing a cape of dirty linen with scrawled on symbols. His eyes ringed in red and black from hitting the pipe, looking every part the king of the junkies.

Her whip slapped hard against her thigh and the girls jumped to attention. She scanned each of them, nodding in satisfaction. All of them ready to fight and scam and cheat and fuck their way out of anything. Teapot was pleased. Slowly she raised a gloved fist to the sky and tipped her head back.

"Let's get fucked up!"

End.

PICKLES

~ 1 0 0 % C U N T ~

By Gregor Cole

EXCERPT:

ONE

CHRIS HAD LOCKED THE BACK DOOR. He checked all the sockets in the kitchen. They were all switched off. Chris made sure there was some food in the bowl for the cat.

He stood at the bottom of the stairs and double checked the television in the front room was off by looking for the red

LED at the bottom of the screen. It was off. A huge weight lifted.

"Can't go wasting energy," He nodded to himself as he climbed the stairs. He was pleased as punch knowing he had a low carbon footprint.

Then began his nightly bathroom routine; cleaning his teeth with *Pure Glisten,* his favourite mild whitening tooth paste. Next he washed his face with *Ned Barker's Tool Shed* masculine face scrub. He clipped away the odd stray nasal hair with his *Simmons's fuzz-be-gone* electric waterproof nostril trimmer. Applying a thin layer of *Manshine* night time moisturiser for men, had made his facial tissue tingle delightfully.

He looked into the mirror and smiled, "There, all done." Chris took his final piss of the day. He flushed, switched off the light and made his way to the bedroom.

He flicked on the 24 hour news with the remote and threw it on to the double king-size bed, before slipping into his bespoke paisley night bottoms.

The sheets were crisp and clean and as he got in it felt like liquid on his tired skin. Chris wriggled into the double thick temper-foam mattress and took a book from the side table, *Fifty Flavours of Vanilla Bean Sex.*

He thumbed the pages, the mediocre soft-core pornography drew too heavy and he was asleep with the book on his belly. The television continued to inform the sleeping man about some war in the Middle East.

Chris began to snore. An inch of drool hung like a slick comma from his bottom lip.

It was the sound of the cat flap on the kitchen door slapping shut that stirred Chris from his slumber. Groggy, he scooped away the sheets sending the trash paperback to the floor.

Chris leaned over to reclaim the dropped book only to brush an oversized shoe with his hand.

At first he thought he was dreaming. There could be no other reason for a giant shoe being there. His hand padded the ground. The only illumination was the gloom from the television light. It was in that he clarified that he was indeed seeing two big shoes that shouldn't have been there.

Chris was sure he was awake.

He rubbed his eyes. Chris sat up only to face the silhouettes of several figures standing in his bedroom. They were smiling as they stared at him.

In a panic he scrambled for the bedside lamp and was sent into a shiver as the light lit a naked female clown. She was standing in the shoes by the side of his bed.

There were seven of them in all; seven naked clown women standing there, watching him rise groggily from sleep.

The clown girl closest to the bed jumped on him, her naked pussy rubbing against his belly as she straddled him. She grabbed his wrists. The other clown women fell on to the bed armed with long thin balloons. They tied them to his feet and arms, thus lashing him to the bed posts.

There was a squeak of rubber as he struggled. It put his teeth on edge and the bonds were way too tight. God, he'd hated balloons. The feel of them, the noise they made when they were blown up but most of all the anticipation of them popping.

He was helpless as the clown girls backed away from the bed to reveal a tiny man dressed in a little red army coat and a wee top hat standing in the middle of the room.

"Mr Doyle, I would like to congratulate you on winning our once in a lifetime amazing competition." The little man danced from foot to foot. "We are here to give you you're prize."

"What fucking competition? What the fuck are you fucking freaks babbling about?" Chris spat at the little fellow. "Who are you?"

"How very rude of me Mr Doyle, my name is Ring Master Thumtumbulous and these are my Funny Girls." The little man tipped his hat and waved an arm of presentation toward the face-painted naked women around him. Each struck a sexy pose as his hand went down the line.

"GET THE FUCK OUT OF MY HOUSE!" Chris couldn't contain his panicked anger.

"No, no, no Mr Doyle, you are a winner." The little ring master circled the bed, barely able to see over the mattress. "You were handed a flyer outside the super market concerning our circus and you called the woman that gave it to you... oh, what was it again?" He held his chin in a little display of sarcasm.

One of the clown girls leaned in, "I believe he called her a *freak* Ring Master."

"That was it, a freak!" The little man nodded.

"You are freaks, you retarded fucking midget!" Chris struggled to free himself from the balloons squeaking clutches, but it came to nothing.

"Winnet, Bella, gag the man. I don't want to hear any more of his filth."

The girls dived on to the bed, their tits bouncing in Chris's face. In other circumstances he may we have enjoyed the experience but you just know it's going downhill from here.

The girls forced his mouth open and put in a plastic dental guard, wedging his jaw open. One of the girls pulled a deflated balloon from her neatly shaved pussy. She wore a red clown wig but her pussy was crowned with a tiny blond Mohawk.

He was pinned to the bed by the clown girl in a green wig. The red wigged girl dunked the wet balloon into Chris's prone mouth. She then leaned in almost to kiss him and with one big breath, she blew the balloon up in his maw.

Chris gagged as the inflatable tickled the back of his throat. His stomach turned with the sound and feel of it rubbing his teeth. With the balloon inflated the girls rubbed their tits in his face and stuck their tongues into each other's mouths and giggled.

"That's enough girls, as you were." The little ring master clapped his hands and the two clowns hopped off the bed with a little wiggle of their arses. "Are you ready for you prize, Mr Doyle?"

From behind the rubber he tried to shout 'GO FUCK YOURSELF' but it came out as a weird buzzing hum.

"Good." The little man took a back step. "Girls, show Mr Doyle what he's won!"

Every girl started pulling handfuls of flat balloons from inside themselves, each handful wet with juices from pussy and arse.

"Mr Doyle," the little man danced again, "CONGRATULATIONS!"

The Funny Girls enveloped the bed in a wave of wet pussy and squeaking rubber.

T W O

THE LAST LUMP OF CRYSTALLISED CHEMICAL crackled away inside the burnt up light bulb.

Fingers covered with soot clung to the makeshift pipe as his painted lips sucked out the smoke. The flame from the trembling disposable lighter caught the glitter in his blue afro. His eyes sunk into the smudged grease paint like piss holes in the snow.

Pickles the Clown slumped back into his chair as the smoke worked its magic in his lungs.

The chemical was being absorbed like a sponge by his near to kaput alveolar membrane. It then rushed into the pulmonary capillaries and into his blood stream. The sweet steam hurried towards his brain adding yet another tiny black spot of damage to his grey matter.

His eyes rolled up into his head as his body shivered from the first wave of intoxication and the world around him flushed away.

Pickles was buzzing from his big toe to his last hair follicle. A sensation of euphoric rapture ensued. It was if his entire body was being licked by a million amateur porn starlets. His limp penis twitched with a pulse of stimuli from the drug signalling his return to reality and his eyes rolled back into the real world. The buzz passed as quickly as it had come leaving Pickles a little disorientated but still high as shit. Pickles had voided his bladder into his sweatpants. "Aw, fuck it!"

He got up dizzy with the effects of the junk he had bought from Dominic the pimp earlier that morning and staggered towards the bathroom to fetch a towel. He pulled down the soaked sweatpants and threw them onto a heap of unwashed laundry.

He washed his dick and his inner thighs in the sink with cold water then stared off into the mirror. The grotty bathroom looked like a stained glass window behind his gaunt made-up face as the residual effect of the drug changed his visual perception.

He walked back out into the hallway; he would need cigarettes and some coffee, maybe a hit or two of sleeping tablets. The chemical in his blood would wear off soon enough and the comedown was hard.

Pickles then stepped bare foot into a pile of cold cat shit. He owned a cat; it was in the flat somewhere. He could hear it moving around under the piles of dirty cloths and ripped up porn at night. It had made the hallway stink of piss. Pickles would get through a lot of incense.

He'd leave a bowl of food down for it every now and then and when he would return to check it was always empty... unless he had rats in there and they had eaten the cat's corpse.

Pickles returned to the sink to wash the turd from between his toes when he heard some post get jammed into his letter box. Through the meshed glass of his front door he heard the postman call him a fucking junky. This always pissed Pickles off.

"Fucking junky?" he posed aloud, thinking hard enough to crease the corpse paint on his forehead. "You simple civil servant," Pickles vented, "I'm a CUNT, motherfucker. One hundred percent."

One time he had caught his postman urinating in his doorway. Looking back he should have reported him but didn't as he had been awake for three days and had lost the use of coherent speech. He later got high and forgot about the whole thing and could only really recall it in a series of almost surreal flashbacks.

Pickles would often forget things in that way.

Maybe it is *all the fucking junk I do,* he considered whilst cleaning the cat shite from his crusty heel.

With his newly cleaned foot he padded across the laminate floor of the hall, avoiding the shit this time to where the crumpled mail lay on the door mat. He stooped to pick it up. A task made all the more difficult with all the narcotics messing with his depth perception.

A stack of bills, companies telling him that they would be taking him to court if he didn't pay up some sort of fee. He had these every day; he didn't even need to open them to tell what they were.

"Bills, bills, occupant, bills, and more bi- ... *ohfuckme...* "

His narcotic filled blood froze when his eyes fell on an envelope he recognised. It was one of fine parchment with a single word scrawled on it in fancy black calligraphy; there was no post mark and no stamp. It read *urgent*.

This letter was posted by hand. They were sending for him again and it meant for trouble. It wasn't to be ignored. The consequences were unthinkable.

Pickles staggered back into the front room and slumped onto his sofa. He placed the letter on the cluttered coffee table in front of him and searched for his cigarettes. His fingers shaking, he pulled one from the roughed up box and after a few tries, Pickles lit it with his trusty disposable.

He glared down at the foreboding correspondence.

One the one hand he'd open it, read it, obey the commands therein and get himself into some fine jam. On the other hand he could ignore it and spend the rest of his life looking over his shoulder and submerging himself even that much deeper in the clown underground.

The thought made him shudder.

He drew on his cigarette deeply and snatched up the letter. It was like a plaster on a tender area; if he opened it slowly it would only hurt more.

Pickles tore at the flap and pulled free the letter from inside. The paper was fine and smelt of bubble gum with a water mark resembling a circus big top.

His stomach knotted as he read the letter aloud.

Pickles… you are here by summoned to stand before il

Consiglio Pagliaccio." He drew once more on the cigarette, blowing the smoke from his nostrils at the letter. *"Your expertise in certain fields is need in a matter of great urgency. The time and place will be made known to you by one of our agents in due course.*

Signed,

Patch Theobald,

High Councillor.

Pickles shook his head.

I am fucked.

He dropped the letter to the floor at his feet and stubbed the cigarette into an overflowing ashtray on the table. He flopped back into the sofa and rubbed his hands across his face smudging his makeup further.

A meeting with the High Council of Clowns was the last thing he needed.

Fucked.

THREE

GIBBON WAS TAKING FIVE.

He'd been doing his job for so long now that the shine had worn off a little. Most people thought filming pornography was a dream job but that couldn't be further from the truth.

Especially now that the circumstances had changed.

It had started out great, sure, working with pretty girls and professional studs for the bigger producers. He had worked on some of the best properties and private lots in the business but then the recession hit and hit hard. All but three of the big producers shut down or went to internet only and the money dried up quicker than an aged porn star after the menopause.

Gibbo was lucky; he had caught a break working for this guy that sold to the privet markets. Gibbo copped a sweet deal shooting his own POV movies. He got to bang loads of prostitutes in motels while filming it all with a handheld camera.

Then the strange orders came through like play-rape, beatings, humiliation, piss and shit fun. If it wasn't for the coke habit and medication bills for all the STD's he'd developed over the last two years he would have turned it all down.

But alas, someone has to do the dirty work.

He propped himself up against a self-store container. Gibbo absently scratched his beard to the sounds of two speed freaks roughly stuffing a baseball bat into the anus of a crack head. He heard it all through the thin panelling. Wish he couldn't, but the walls were so thin he could even hear the dudes when they spat in her mouth.

The sound of a punch to the crack whore's stomach made him gag a little as he smoked and scratched.

~VENGEANCE OF THE VIGILANTE ROLLER SLUTS~

By the time the rhythmical slapping of nutsack against wet arsehole started he was sitting in his car going through the glove box. Gibbo was looking for his .38 pistol.

Sweat rolled down his forehead and he pulled his shoulder length hair back into a little nub on the back of his head.

He turned on the radio. Neil Diamond. He turned off the radio.

Gibbon had lost count the amount of times he had put that barrel into his mouth and tickled the trigger He'd never managed to pluck up the courage to squeeze. Gibbo often wanted something to startle him so he would accidently blow the back of his skull all over the interior of his shit box Volvo.

The gun had a strange taste, like off milk. Gibbo put that down to the amount of dried saliva that was inside the barrel. He had never cleaned the thing and only ever fired it once at a road sign to see if it worked.

The kick of it gave him a start and because he was a little high he nearly shit in his pants from the sound. He had left it in his car ever since but every now and then he would sit there, with it in his mouth, waiting for someone to knock on the window out of the blue.

Gibbo pulled it free from his lips; a string of drool formed a bridge from his bottom lip to the raised sight in the barrel. He peered down the black hole of the gun and wondered what it would look like if it went off in his face.

Would he feel if? Wondered Gibbon.

Would he even give a fuck?

He slumped over the searing wheel face down with his arms flopped over the dash, the drool now dribbling from his mouth down to the sticky mat in the foot-well. He let it happen. He had no shame by this point.

He wondered whether the speed freaks had killed the crack whore. He wondered if he would care if they had.

The sound of someone knocking on his passenger window caused him to jump. He clenched his hands instinctively and the .38 spat a lump of hot lead through his windscreen, accompanied by a deafening clap.

In a panic he screamed and dropped the gun. It went off again sending a bullet into the engine block of the car and again with an ear splitting bang. He grabbed for the door and fell out onto the gravel. The person that had knocked on the window was cowering on the other side of the colour miss-matched vehicle.

"For fuck sake, Gibbo, what the fuck was that?"
Gibbo recognised the voice through the ringing in his ears. It was Ruby, one of the girls he worked with. She specialised in oversized insertions and her gimmick was clown make-up. Gibbo had shot a lot of clown porn.

Almost too much.

~VENGEANCE OF THE VIGILANTE ROLLER SLUTS~

Her head popped up over the roof of the car. Ruby's purple hair pulled up into a pineapple. Her face was white with perfect red circles on her cheeks. One eye painted with a green diamond, the other a blue triangle. The thick red of her lips looked like her head was split in two.

"You're not going to try and kill me are you?" She waved to Gibbon who just stared up at the sky.

"No, you're okay; I was just having a meditative moment, honey." He rolled over and crawled his way over to the car and used it to climb to his feet, "Nothing to worry about, just one of those days." Ruby hopped around the car to help him dust down.

The door of the container was flung open and one of the speed freaks stuck his head out to see what the commotion was. Gibbo waved him away like a bad smell and the door soon slammed shut in a huff.

How dare they interrupt their crack whore cunt whipping?

"Fucking junkies," Ruby shook her head, "can't fucking stand those pricks, get off hurting girls. They'd kill 'em if they thought they could."

"Yeah, but it pays the bills, honey." Gibbon reached into the car and shoved the pistol back into the glove box. "I just let them get on with it now. What they do is totally down to them."

"But they are still fucking sick."

~GREGOR COLE~

"Tell me about it. I have the lovely job of editing four different cameras worth of their rape footage later on today, but only after I have the pleasure of your company, honey."

"Aw, thank you Gibbo, you make it sound so nice."

"Yeah, I'm a real sweetheart." He took a cigarette from his shirt pocket and scratched at his thick beard again. "Anyhow, those pricks will be done in a minute then we can set up."

As Ruby was about to give the big lunk a huge hug a white van with fat tyres and wide arches rolled up on the gravel drive. Its big V8 engine thumped as the vehicle came sliding to a stop on the loose surface, kicking up a cloud of dust as it did so.

The windscreen was tinted but they could still make out a figure; one with a big blue afro and mirrored aviator sunglasses. Grindcore blasted out from inside the tank-like van sending vibrations through the metal panels. It caused something to vibrate at the same frequency of the fat riffs and a crack in the window buzzed with the bass line.

The van stopped and the driver jumped down from his high driving position. He wore cut-down combat shorts, a black and white pair of high-tops and a t-shirt with *100% CUNT* on the front in big white letters.

They both recognised who it was straight away. It was Pickles.

Fuck.

He was outside on a weekday.

He wasn't expected and he wasn't here to pick up drugs.

That meant trouble.

Fucked.

FOUR

"SO WHAT BRINGS YOU HERE, GOOD BUDDY?" Gibbo had thrown out the stars of his last movie and finished wiping the secretions from the furniture. The odour of crack smoke and anal sex still lingered no matter how much lavender air freshener he sprayed.

"Well, I've come for Ruby." Pickles expression was dour.

"I ain't going anywhere, I have a scene to shoot then I'm getting my nails done." Ruby sat with on a beanbag in the corner of the coverted container. Her arms were crossed like a petulant child

"Fuck your nails, bitch," Pickles was not happy at the reply and glared through his aviators at the sulking girl. "I've been called in to see the council."

The room was quiet for a moment, like Gibbo's gun had gone off by accident again. It was Gibbo that broke the silence.

"That can't be anything good."

"No, it can't." Pickles was still staring at Ruby. "So I'm

going to need some help."

"I'm not going." Ruby huffed.

"I'm not asking."

"Good."

Pickles leaned in a little closer to where Ruby was sulking. "I'm fucking telling."
Ruby looked almost shocked at the audacity of the dirty junky fuck. Who was he to bark orders, after all jams she had got him out of.

"A fucking washed up clown telling me what to do, who the fuck do you think…"

"I'm the guy that stopped Dingo Jack from raping your arse, beating you and leaving you dead in my place, you ungrateful whore." Pickles flopped back into his seat, he had played his hand.

"You can't bring that up." Rube looked like she might cry.

"I can and I have."

"That's dark, Pickles man, you know she's grateful for that, we all are." Gibbo was almost on the verge of smashing the clowns face in but knew if the council was calling it was for a good reason. "Why do they want you in, or is it the usual hush-hush operation?"

"Don't know, don't care, usual bullshit, information or some sort of favour, but I'm going to need support." Pickles took off his sun glasses. His blood-shot eyes were ringed with black make-up. "I'm in a bad way and need a little help… mentally."

"You do look messed up." Ruby got to her feet, her face instantly change to one of gloating joy. "Hitting that glass dick a little too hard, eh?"

"Fuck you, cum bucket." Pickles rubbed at his eyes, letting the lies roll off his tongue. "Nothing I haven't been through before."

"Really, because you look fucked to me."

"Ruby, the man's going through some shit, we've all been there." Gibbo pulled up a chair in front of Pickles. "Now when you say mental, what level are we talking?"

"Oh, the normal shit: the fear, visual interference, scared of the outside world, mild uncontrollable hallucinations. You know, nothing too bad but enough to worry."

"So back-up is needed then." Gibbo scratched at his beard again and turned to Ruby. "I think you might give the guy a break, honey."

"I dunno, this guy is just trouble and I don't trust him."

"Look you can either help me out or I can explain to the council that I turned to a sister for help and she turned me down, even out in the sticks they can make it hard for you to get work." Pickles wiped the sweat from his brow. "The rumour of venereal disease in the ear of the right people and they'll drop you quicker than a burning turd. You'll have to play the game for real. There'll be no more picking and choosing, just like this chump." He threw a thumb at Gibbo who nodded woefully.

"He's right, honey. The council could shut you done real fast, you'll end up like that crack head bitch getting destroyed for food stamps and rock hits."

Ruby's face dropped as the realisation that they were right set in. She was cute but a few months on the perv circuit would sort that out. A few black eyes, the occasional broken finger and a couple of swift kicks in the crotch wouldn't help her one bit and the mere sniff of VD would instantly put her in the junky category. Fair game. Open season. All the slime would be after her then.

The girls that worked in those circles never lasted too long. They usually turned to the junk. Or else they'd end up being found under a plastic sheet somewhere by old folks walking their four-legged shit machine.

She knew what side her bread was buttered.

"So if I help you this one time does that mean you'll owe me a pretty big favour?"

"Yeah, I guess so. That's if I last long enough to owe you." Pickles reluctantly nodded. "So you'll help?"

"Any favour, no matter how big?" Ruby was getting anxious.

"What, like caving in a rapist's skull for you?"

"Fuck sake, Pickles." Gibbo leaned back in his chair.

"You're never letting that go are you?" Ruby was still not happy that he couldn't let it go.

"All I'm saying is I will owe you to the point of putting someone in a wheelchair for life…again!"

Gibbo looked worried and stared at Ruby when he asked. "So when's all this going down, when's the meet?"

"Dunno, they said I will be approached by an agent, whatever that means."

"Well you better get your shit together then." Gibbo got up and started to tinker with a large VHS camera on a tripod. "And you young lady have a scene to shoot, so if you don't mind Pickles, I don't care if you stay I just don't want you in the way."

Pickles did as he was told and plonked himself down on the beanbag in the corner as Gibbo set up for the shoot. Pickles was nearly blinded by the redhead lamp Gibbo switched on that was attached to the celling of the container. It burnt at his retinas like branding irons and he was forced to put his sunglasses back on.

Ruby meanwhile stripped down to her birthday suit and tied her hair up. She then rifled through her bag of props. Both men's jaws dropped as she produced an inflatable rubber chicken from the duffle bag.

She made her way to a grotty little mattress propped up on a stack of shipping pallets. Ruby hopped up on to the makeshift bed and spread her legs wide exposing her thin lipped pussy to the camera.

"Gibbo, be a love and get some lube from my bag. I might need it for my arse."

Class, Pickles thought. *All class.*

End excerpt.

'click' on cover image to get your this and other Gregor Cole Kindle copies today!

ABOUT THE SICK AND TWISTED GREGOR COLE:

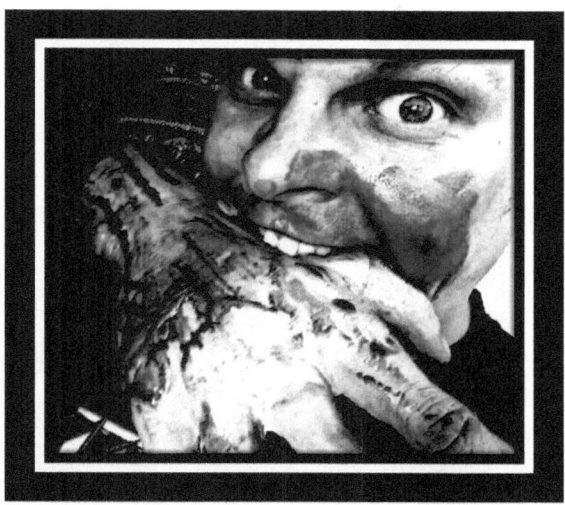

Gregor Cole works out of Kent (the garden of England) in the UK spending most of his free time scribbling away in the gloom and watching classic horror.

He sharpens the knives of his craft on a diet of tea, biscuits and lemon loaf cake, constantly waiting for the postman to deliver his weekly selection of gore films and bizarro literature.

ALSO AVAILABLE FROM Morbidbook**S**
IN PRINT & KINDLE:

(click on images for hyper-links)

FROM ALEX S. JOHNSON, THE AUTHOR OF BAD SUNSET, Wicked Candy and The Death Jazz, comes a new vision in Bizarro horror. Imagine a TROMA film on meth and acid, one part cyberpunk, one part Franz Kafka, and three parts frankly unsuitable for a sane audience. "Will make you feel as if you've just eaten 8 Percocets and washed 'em down with a bottle of moonshine," says Necro Stein of Texas Terror Entertainment.

WHEN THE WINDS BLEW I FELT THEM BLOWING THROUGH me, when the land shook, it was my corpus that trembled. When the tides ebbed and flowed I became more shore and more sea. I was day and night as the sun and moon described the steps of their dancing within me. Just as I could see all the world at once, I was all of these things at once, and the motion of an entire world formed the foundation of my stillness.

I'd travelled through the Sphere of Glammeth, descended through the Guardian, and then through the Grey-Man, fallen through a hole that pierced all the worlds. I had followed the stream to its source and become the worlds through which I'd fallen; now in completion I dwelt in gaps between overlapping pulses of time; the multitude within the one.

Whole in content, whole in process, whole in time. Seeing all, being all, my eyes the eyes of the cosmos, in ultimate being.

~GREGOR COLE~

HE HAD TO HAVE HER THE MOMENT HE SAW HER TRACHEA ring. Six months later she was his lovely wife. He performed his duties as a husband and she as a wife. He tolerated a house filled with references to her late first husband and the children they had together. He put up with her prudish ways. He waited. He was patient. He planned. He was adaptable. He was rewarded over the course of a week in her basement. He turned his perverse sexual fantasies of worms and maggots and her lovely crusty trachea ring into a gruesome reality.

A DIRTY SHAMEFUL DEVIL OF A SECRET...

Something that two men share. A legacy that will shock you to your very core. One that is created not out of madness, but of the purest desire. Take a vivid journey into the mind of the killer and his biggest fan. Do you believe in evil? See the knife plunge. Lap at the wounds. Do you still? There is no rational meaning or pretty words that will hide away the darkness that the words of this found journal creates. Inside is the real truth. And it can set you free. Watch all you want. Taste what you dare not have. But once you see, you are in collusion. Keep reading and the guilt will stain. No longer can you feign innocence. The change is as permanent as it is wretched. Perhaps you should just walk away. This shit right here is a MorbidbookS blunt. You dig?

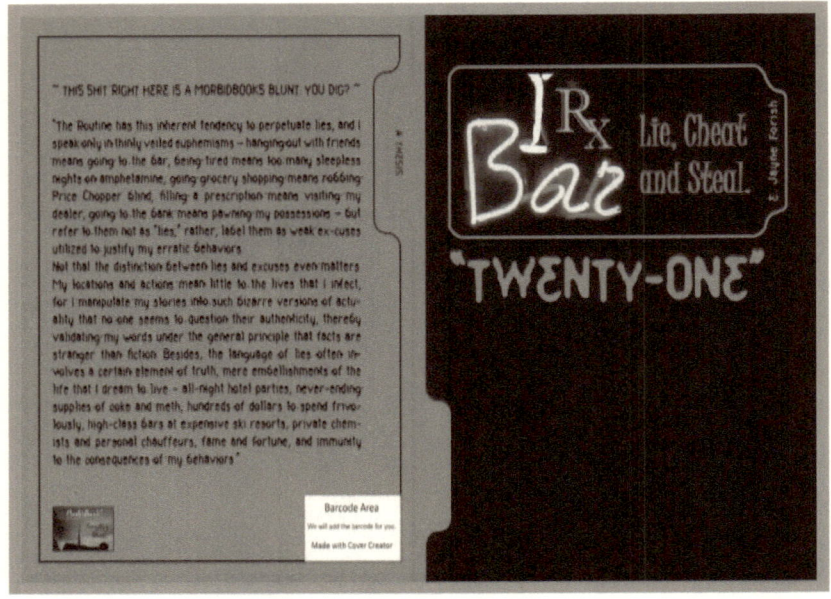

"THE ROUTINE HAS THIS INHERENT TENDENCY TO perpetuate lies, and I speak only in thinly veiled euphemisms — hanging out with friends means going to the bar; being tired means too many sleepless nights on amphetamine; going grocery shopping means robbing Price Chopper blind; filling a prescription means visiting my dealer; going to the bank means pawning my possessions — but refer to them not as "lies;" rather, label them as weak excuses utilized to justify my erratic behaviors.

Not that the distinction between lies and excuses even matters. My locations and actions mean little to the lives that I infect, for I manipulate my stories into such bizarre versions of actuality that no one seems to question their authenticity, thereby validating my words under the general principle that facts are stranger than fiction. Besides, the language of lies often involves a certain element of truth, mere embellishments of the life that I dream to live – all-night hotel parties, never-ending supplies of coke and meth, hundreds of dollars to spend frivolously, high-class bars at expensive ski resorts, private chemists and personal chauffeurs, fame and fortune, and immunity to the consequences of my behaviours."

HUMANITY IS THE DEVIL IS A DECONSTRUCTED NIGHTMARE mixing David Lynch and snuff movies. The plot revolves around a central character, Seth, who is set about a crusade against humanity which, for him, represents pure evil. Through random killings he and his cronies try to accelerate the end of the world, in order to provoke and defeat the Demiurge, the false God that is ruling the earth. As in Burroughs, logical language is replaced here with cut-scenes – sometimes to be taken literally – that plunge the reader into an extreme experience. Both incredibly

~GREGOR COLE~

morbid and enthralling, HITD is a masterpiece of moral darkness and existentialist reflection upon our comfortable religion and morals.

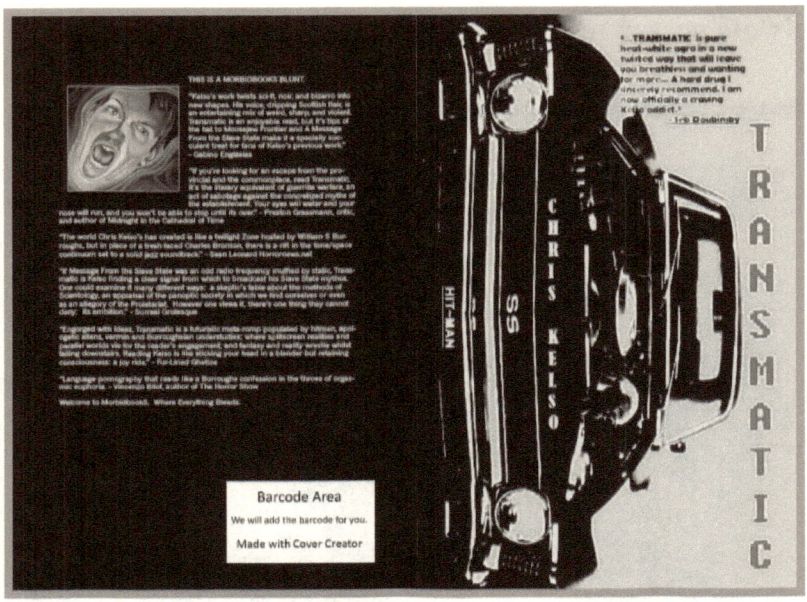

"AS A PART-TIME HITMAN/ EXTERMINATOR, Ignius Ellis's dream is to buy a candy-apple red Nova Supreme. In the process of trying to earn enough cash to make his dream come true he gets sucked into the rough world of Visitacion Valley, SF. When the tenants in his apartment complex reveal their various extracurricular activities this take an even more bizarre twist and Ellis soon becomes acquainted with the nightmarish Slave State dimension..."

THAT'S THE LAST TIME SHE GETS THE BIGGER WORM... Once their flesh flakes away the angels collapse into puddles of hissing goop and withered petals blow into them hurried along by unseen winds. My spit looses its sweet taste to the black flavor of ash. The glowing birds in the bright orange sky burst into small sparkly novas. The sky itself weeps and tears, streaking down like a ruined painting as the dismal gray of life wheezes back before my eyes. I don't blink; praying silently for one last desperate sensation of the high. Lila feels it too. She writhes on the mattress next to me; her moans of ecstasy warping into groans that capture the hollowness of our souls. Tears form in her eyes and I can almost feel the lump in her throat. It's gone and she wants to cry. I'd rather chase down more Worms than cry about it but everybody reacts to the Worms differently. I slip away to my own neon colored utopia

~GREGOR COLE~

where things with wings fan me and comfort me when the living neon worm dissolves under my skin. Lila told me once they wrap around her like a giant fuzzy neon hug. I imagine her high shedding off her like snake skin and flaking to the filthy floor next to the mattress. Her high sounds better than mine. More Fun. That's the last time she gets the bigger worm.

"**IF YOU KNOW WHAT KINBAKU, POST-IMPRESSIONISM**, and brilliant green eyes have in common, then you are probably a fan of Alex S. Johnson! Congrats! But if you don't know, allow me to open the door, guide you inside, and introduce you to a little Wicked Candy. This is a sweet designed for the discerning Bizzarro fan's tastes, and I promise, you will not be disappointed!"

--Mimi Williams, author of Beautiful Monster

~VENGEANCE OF THE VIGILANTE ROLLER SLUTS~

"A short collection that both traverses the genre lines and melds them together into one masterpiece. Jam packed with horror, laughs, pop culture history and more, this one is a must have for lovers of the macabre, the bizarre and the hilarious."

--Jeff O'Brien, author of Bigboobenstein

IN GARRETT COOK'S MURDERLAND serial killers are idolized by society. Their deeds are followed obsessively by television pundits and the adoring public. A subculture has grown up around this phenomena, called "Reap." Laws are created to allow this activity to flourish, including designated "safe zones' where killers can practice their trade without fear of persecution. Fans of the top rated serial killers celebrate each new kill on social media and television. Programs glorify their deeds.

The culture of Murderland is violent and mirrors our own

~GREGOR COLE~

violent society and its decadent obsessions; but Murderland isn't about how violent the world has become. It's about the pervasive nature of media and how it corrupts. It corrupts absolutely.

At the heart of Murderland is Jeremy Jenkins. Jeremy doesn't like what he sees and he's just enough insane to believe he can do something about it, that he can change the world. His methods are extreme- to outdo the serial killers, he'll kill THEM, turn their own twisted reality back on themselves. It's a hopeless task, impossible, Herculean; but it's Jeremy's fate to see it through to the end.

The three sections of Murderland comprise a true Homeric epic. In the first section we are shown the terrible world Jeremy lives in, the world that if we look at it honestly, is really our own world. We meet all the principal characters, the serial killers, the pundits, the pawns, and Jeremy's beloved Cass. In the second section Jeremy goes on a bit of a spiritual quest and comes to understand his true purpose. In the final section the flames are ignited and all hell breaks loose. Jeremy, like a great epic hero must journey to the underworld and be reborn in order to triumph.

BORN WHOLE FROM THE RECTUM of a dying patient, Morbid silently stalks the hospital's hallways, heinously dispatching the most helpless of patients and in the most painfully repulsive of manners. In the meantime, in order to pay for his family and home that includes his ghost step-father Sammy and his pet aborted fetus Chip, Westphal has to ingest mounds of dangerous narcotics to get through his night shifts. Barely hanging on to his Care Tech gig by his fingernails, the last thing Westphal needs is to be accused of Morbid's evil deeds. You, on the other hand, simply want to find some solace. Terminally ill from a virulent infection, and dependent on Life Support, all You beg for a peaceful and dignified demise. Shirk has other plans for You. The ancient drug-snuffling demon makes You relive all of your deadly and venial sins as he tortures You. Night after night. Until eternal Damnation begins for YOU MORBID WESTPHAL, yet again.... NOW WITH EVEN *MORE* EVIL FLAVOR!

~GREGOR COLE~

IT LOOKS LIKE CAROLYN AND MARK are in deep, deep shit... Mark and Carolyn live in an alternate 1989 where Ronald Reagan is on his fourth presidential term. The USA has a rigid, long-standing caste system and abortions were never made legal. Being homeless is a crime that is punishable by imprisonment in an internment camp the inmates call Tent City. Most of Mark's ER patients are inmates at this camp and are victims of a new disease these illegals call the Transient Flu. This deadly and rapidly spreading disease mutates with each new host, collecting information, changing code. The disease evolves lightning quick, spreading like pond ripples and infecting everyone. No one is safe. Mark and Carolyn dig too deep and uncover the brutal truth: Transient Flu was purposely made and is one hundred percent fatal. Carolyn's employer, Hudson-

~VENGEANCE OF THE VIGILANTE ROLLER SLUTS~

Smythe Pharmaceuticals, discovers the chain of evidence. It traces the pharmacide back to Hudson–Smythe and the crime of the century. Cost is no object and deadly force is authorized. Yes. Carolyn and Mark are in deep, deep shit.

IMMANUEL THE CHRIST HAS SOME NERVE. Jonah has already lost everyone he loves to Pilate the vampire and his Harbor drug violence. Jonah now trudges through his days staying as high on Plata as possible. He just wants to be left alone while he waits for his turn to die. The Christ has other plans for him. She sends Her messenger, Pedro, to assign Jonah the very dangerous task of ordering the Herod to dismantle the Harbor's Plata trade. Jonah decides to run. But you can't run from God forever. As Jonah learns the hard way when the 'Edmund Fitzgerald' founders and goes down in rough seas, with the reluctant prophet on board.

~GREGOR COLE~

Job is Satan's Chosen One and he doesn't take kindly to orders from some upstart prophet. Rather than acquiescing, Job thinks caving Jonah's head in with a tire iron is the best bet. Jonah finds himself out of the frying pan, but firmly fixed in the fire. Then the Lord Herself starts dispatching Job's children. One at a time, until the Herod of The Harbor finally obeys.